SECRETS OF
BEARHAVEN

BOOK TWO

MISSION TO
MOON FARM

SECRETS OF
BEARHAVEN

BOOK TWO

MISSION TO
MOON FARM

K. E. ROCHA

SCHOLASTIC PRESS / NEW YORK

Library of Congress Cataloging-in-Publication Data

Names: Rocha, K. E., author.
Title: Mission to Moon Farm / K.E. Rocha.
Description: First edition. | New York, NY : Scholastic Press, 2016. | Series:
    Secrets of Bearhaven ; Book two | Summary: Spencer Plain has been settling
    into his new home in Bearhaven, the secret refuge his parents created, learning
    to speak Ragayo which is the bear's language, and improving his survival
    skills—he still does not know where his parents are, but he knows that when
    his best friend, a bear cub named Kate, is kidnapped it is up to him to rescue
    her before it is too late.
Identifiers: LCCN 2016016963| ISBN 9780545813044
Subjects: LCSH: Bears—Juvenile fiction. | Human-animal communication—
    Juvenile fiction. | Kidnapping—Juvenile fiction. | Best friends—Juvenile
    fiction. | Rescues—Juvenile fiction. | CYAC: Bears—Fiction. | Human-animal
    communication—Fiction. | Kidnapping—Fiction. | Best friends—Fiction. |
    Friendship—Fiction. | Rescues—Fiction.
Classification: LCC PZ7.1.R637 Mi 2016 | DDC [Fic]—dc23 LC record
    available at https://lccn.loc.gov/2016016963

10 9 8 7 6 5 4 3 2 1   16 17 18 19 20

Printed in the U.S.A. 23
First edition, September 2016

Book design by Nina Goffi

For Barbara Ferguson Young

1

Spencer Plain raced down the wooden dock. His eyes were glued to the bear cub in the river. He had to get her out of there, and fast. He could practically hear the clock ticking in his head.

The bear gave a feeble kick, fighting the current that threatened to carry her downriver. Spencer took a flying leap and launched himself off the end of the dock. He plunged into the cold water, kicked back up to the surface, and swam as hard as he could straight at the bear. As soon as Spencer reached the cub, he clamped one arm around her and started back toward shore.

Thank goodness she's just a cub, Spencer thought. His muscles were straining. He wasn't sure he'd be able to swim at all if she was any bigger.

Something scratched his arm, his lungs were burning, and sopping wet chestnut-colored fur kept getting in his eyes. Spencer ignored all of it. He couldn't let anything distract him from getting the cub out of the water *now.* He swam as hard as he could until his feet connected with the riverbed. *Almost there!* Spencer pulled the bear through the shallow water, then collapsed on the shore.

"Time!" a voice called from the dock.

Spencer sat up, trying to catch his breath. Beside him, Kate Weaver, his bear cub best friend, popped up to all fours. She gave a huge shake of her fur and drenched Spencer in a fresh coat of river water. She had mastered her drowning act in order to make Spencer's river rescue training feel more real, but now the training exercise was over. She didn't have to pretend she was in deep trouble anymore.

"You did *great*, Spencer!" Kate exclaimed. Spencer shook water out of his ear, relieved. Even though he knew Kate hadn't really been in danger, he always felt better when the exercise was finished and she returned to her playful, enthusiastic self. Kate scooped up a nearby towel in her teeth and swung her head toward Spencer, offering it to him.

"Thanks, Kate." He took the towel. "I think your BEAR-COM got me again," he added, showing her the scratch on his arm.

"I'm sorry." The cub dipped her snout up close to the pink scratch. Her eyes were wide.

Spencer shrugged. He didn't want Kate to feel bad. "It's okay. It's kind of like a battle wound." He glanced over at the BEAR-COM fastened around her neck, the only sparkly BEAR-COM in Bearhaven. The high-tech device translated the growls of the bears' language, Ragayo, into English. Kate had decorated her BEAR-COM with pink crystals, and those crystals kept scratching Spencer during river rescues.

It wasn't like he could ask Kate to take her BEAR-COM off during his training. Without it, they wouldn't have any way of talking to each other. At least not the way they could now. Kate had taught Spencer a few words in Ragayo, but without those phrases, and without the BEAR-COM, they wouldn't get very far in these rescue training sessions.

"Don't worry, it's just a scratch." Spencer moved his arm away from Kate's inspection.

"If you say so!" Her enthusiasm returned. "That was your fastest river rescue yet! Right, Aldo?" she called to her older brother, Spencer's training tutor. The much larger black bear was padding down the riverbank toward them. Aldo was carrying Spencer's backpack in his mouth and couldn't answer.

Spencer jumped to his feet and rushed over to take the backpack. He was too excited to hear if he'd broken his river rescue record to wait any longer.

"You're definitely getting faster, Spencer," Aldo answered once he'd released the bag from between his jaws. "That was fifty-eight seconds. Well done."

"You beat your record!" Kate cheered.

"Finally!" Spencer had been training after school all week and up to now hadn't been able to get Kate to shore in under a minute. He couldn't wait to record his new time.

"Finally? I'd say you're a pretty quick learner, little man. And, Kate," Aldo went on, "your bear-in-need-of-rescue performance has gotten too convincing. I almost jumped in to save you myself." The bear nuzzled his little sister playfully.

Kate took a goofy, four-legged bow. "Spencer is training to be an operative, but *I'm* training to star in the next Bearhaven play."

Spencer laughed as he dug around in his backpack, pushing aside his sneakers and T-shirt. He imagined the cub taking her bow in the middle of a brightly lit stage. The idea was less crazy to him now than it would have been two weeks ago. Two weeks ago, he hadn't even known that Bearhaven, a secret community of rescued bears and their families, existed. Now he was living in it.

Spencer's hand closed around the notebook he'd been searching for. He pulled it out, then grabbed a pen from the backpack's front pocket.

STORM was written in big bold letters across the front of Spencer's training notebook. He flipped to the first page, where he and Aldo had outlined the skills Spencer would need to master in order to become an operative. The list was based on exercises Bearhaven's security squad, the Bear Guard, had to do in their own training.

Aldo was a new member of the guard himself, with the silver cuffs on his front legs to prove it. Spencer wouldn't get cuffs when he completed his training, because he wasn't trying to become an actual member of the Bear Guard. He was training so he could become a human operative and get approval to go on bear rescue missions. He'd go with a team of other operatives to save bears from dangerous places and evil people who treated them badly. Then he'd help bring the bears to Bearhaven, following in his parents' footsteps and joining them in the bear rescue work they had been doing for Spencer's whole life. The only thing was: Spencer had no idea about his mom and dad's work until two weeks ago when their disappearance from a bear rescue mission had landed him here.

Spencer tried not to think about the fact that his parents' whereabouts were still a mystery. Everyone kept telling him

Mom and Dad were closer than ever to making it back to Bearhaven. They told him he didn't need to worry. But aside from STORM training and going to school with Kate, there wasn't much that could truly distract him from thinking about his missing parents.

Spencer turned his attention back to his notebook, flipping through it. Each section started with a big bold letter that stood for one part of his training. *S* was for stealth, *T* for tree climbing, *O* for operative communications, *R* for river rescues, and *M* for muscle. He turned back to the *R* section of the notebook and wrote *58 seconds* on the next empty line, along with the date.

"Sun's setting, you two. I have to get to a guard workout soon," Aldo said. "How about you run home, Spencer. Record it in the 'Muscle' section. Kate can set a pace for you."

"Okay. Thanks for—"

"What pace?" Kate interrupted. "Fast, slow, or in the middle?" She always took her part in Spencer's training very seriously. The cub was just as dedicated to Spencer becoming an operative as he was.

"Between in the middle and fast," Aldo answered, giving Kate something to puzzle over for the next few minutes.

Spencer returned his training notebook to his backpack and pulled on his T-shirt. He laced up his sneakers, then got to his feet and slung his backpack over his shoulder. "Hey Aldo, stealth or operative communications tomorrow?"

"Let's give tree climbing another try."

"Oh." Of all the things Spencer did in STORM training, tree climbing was his least favorite.

"On your marks," Aldo said. Obviously, tomorrow's training wasn't up for discussion. Kate rushed over to get into position beside Spencer, her eyes already zeroing in on the path that led into the center of Bearhaven, toward the Weavers' home.

"Get set."

Spencer took a deep breath. He didn't know how Kate would interpret Aldo's instructions, but he was determined to stay with her, no matter how fast she decided to go.

"GO!" Aldo cried from behind them. Spencer took off running. In the same instant, a chestnut-colored streak of fur flew out ahead of him.

"A little slower! Closer to in the middle!" Aldo yelled, but it was too late. Kate was setting the pace, and that pace was *fast*.

2

Spencer burst through the Weavers' front door a few paces behind Kate. He didn't slow down as he careened into the large, honey-colored room. Instead, he sped up and, using his last little bit of energy, hurtled over the armrest of the closest couch. He stretched out midair and belly flopped onto bear-sized cushions.

"Nice!" someone called. Spencer's body sank into the soft couch. He lay there for a second, catching his breath after the hard run back from the river. There were things about Bearhaven Spencer knew he'd miss when he went back to his real home. Entering a room by belly flopping onto an extra-large couch was *definitely* one of them.

Spencer swung his feet to the ground and stood up. Winston and Jo-Jo Weaver were in the kitchen, arranging wooden plates around the table for dinner. The "nice" comment had to have come from one of them.

Winston and Jo-Jo were two more of Kate's brothers. Unlike Aldo, they weren't older than Kate by very much, and it showed. For one thing, they weren't as big as Aldo yet. For another, they were the ones who'd taught Spencer the belly flop move. At first, Spencer had thought Winston and Jo-Jo were tricking him by teaching him something that would only get him in trouble. But then their mom, Bunny Weaver, had walked into the room during the tutorial, and she hadn't minded the belly flops at all. Cubs were always allowed to run and climb on things like they would in the wild, and couches were just the same to them as trees and boulders.

"I'm glad to see some of your training is paying off, Spencer. But I'm going to guess Aldo didn't teach you that move," said Lisle Weaver, the eldest of the Weaver siblings, who was in the kitchen, piling wooden platters high with food.

"Winston and Jo-Jo taught him," Kate chimed in. She'd already taken her seat at the table and was resting her muzzle on the stone surface. Her brown snout was only inches from a platter of troutloaf, a dish Spencer knew tasted something like fish sticks and meatloaf combined. Some of the bears' food was delicious, but Spencer wouldn't put troutloaf in that category.

"They did," Spencer agreed as he slid off his backpack and dropped it beside the couch. He was surprised to see Lisle putting dinner on the table. Usually, Bunny was in charge of dinner, and Lisle spent most evenings with Fitch, her father's assistant and the bear she was going to marry at the end of the summer.

"So did you learn how to get insects out of a log in school today, Spencer?" Jo-Jo teased, making space on the table for Lisle's platters of food. He and Winston loved to poke fun at Spencer for attending the bears' school.

"Actually . . . yeah, I did," Spencer answered. He didn't mind the teasing. It wasn't like he had any choice: Professor

Weaver and Uncle Mark told him he had to attend school with the cubs. Besides, learning about bear stuff from real bears was pretty cool, and it certainly beat his sixth grade science class back home.

"Just wait," said Winston. "Right now you're the only human in our school, but by the time you leave Bearhaven, you'll be the only bear in your human school!"

"Where are Mom and Dad?" Kate asked, moving her snout away from the troutloaf just long enough to sniff for her parents. Spencer glanced around the large room. It was split into two spaces: one half was the family room, where he stood now, with couches arranged around a huge fireplace; in the other half of the room was a massive stone kitchen. Off the kitchen, a bear-sized set of stairs led down to the lower level of the Weavers' house. *Professor Weaver and Bunny must not be here,* Spencer realized when neither of the Weaver parents appeared at the top of the steps for dinner.

"They were called to a last-minute Bear Council meeting." Lisle said. "Ready for dinner, Spencer?"

"Thanks, Lisle," Spencer said, sitting down between Lisle and Kate. Beside Spencer's wooden plate there was a fork, knife, and spoon. He was the only one who needed utensils. The bears used their claws to spear things, or they just put their mouths to their food and ate.

"You're welcome. Eat up, everyone."

After two weeks in Bearhaven, Spencer was starting to recognize the different dishes the Weavers served. Tonight they were having troutloaf, moss slaw, berry cakes, and tons of salad. The bears dug in. Spencer reached for a berry cake. Winston did the same.

"Yikes!" Spencer jerked his hand back just in time to avoid a painful run-in with Winston's claws.

"Oops," Winston growled, spearing the berry cake he'd been eyeing. "Sorry, Spencer." The bear chomped the berry cake off his claw and gulped it down, then reached to fill his plate with food.

"It's okay." Spencer was glad not to have lost a finger. "I'll just wait until you guys finish getting your food."

Once the bears turned their attention from the platters of food to eating the heaping portions on their own plates, Spencer served himself.

"What's the Bear Council meeting about?" he asked, helping himself to a very little bit of troutloaf.

"They didn't say." Lisle tilted her head. "The Bear Council tends to keep things under wraps." Spencer knew all about that. The Bear Council was the group of Bearhaven's wisest, most important bears. They made all the major decisions for the community, but their meetings were almost always restricted to council members only. Just getting into their meeting room was nearly impossible if you weren't a member. Spencer had managed to break the rules and get in there once before, but not everyone had been very happy about that.

Spencer started to ask if Lisle thought the meeting might be about Mom and Dad, but Kate was already changing the subject.

"Spencer, if your parents get back to Bearhaven tomorrow, will you leave right away?"

"Um . . ." Spencer didn't know what to say. For a second, the idea of Mom and Dad walking through the Weavers' front door tomorrow made him so happy he couldn't think of anything else.

"Well, will you?" Kate pushed.

"I don't know." Spencer shrugged. He didn't want to disappoint Kate, but when Mom and Dad finally did get to Bearhaven, Spencer thought they would all leave for home together right away. "But even if I do, I'll come back to Bearhaven," he added. "I'll have to finish my operative training, and after that, I'll come back all the time so I can use my training and go on bear rescue missions with my parents."

"You won't miss my concert though, will you?" Kate asked. "No matter what?"

"Nope," Spencer answered. "There's no way I'm missing that." He filled his mouth with a big bite of salad so he couldn't say any more.

"*Your* concert?" Jo-Jo exclaimed.

"Since when did it become *your* concert?" said Winston.

Kate rolled her eyes dramatically. Spencer shoveled more salad into his mouth to hide his grin. Winston and Jo-Jo were right: Kate was really only one member of the Weaver Family Singers. Winston, Jo-Jo, Aldo, Lisle, and Bunny would all be up there together, singing with her when the family band performed their concert in Bearhaven's town center.

"Oh, leave her alone." Lisle shook her head at her younger brothers. "Kate's just excited about her first solo."

"SOLO!" Winston hooted. "It's just ten words in the middle of the song!"

"It's *twelve* words," Kate huffed. "Twelve words that I sing *alone*. As in *solo*."

Winston and Jo-Jo rolled off their seats they were laughing so hard. The second their paws hit the ground, they were tripping over each other, racing toward the stairs.

"Thanks for dinner, Lisle!" Jo-Jo called over his shoulder. "I have to go show Winston what it means to bow down to the Salmon King!"

"No way!" Winston yelled over his brother as they thundered down the stairs.

"Well, I'm glad *they're* gone," Kate said, once the clamoring of paws had quieted.

"Oh, Spencer!" Lisle exclaimed as she stood up from the table. "I was waiting to tell you, your uncle Mark isn't going to be able to call tonight. He's in the council meeting, too." The silver-colored bear started to clear the table using her mouth and the special handles that were attached to each of the now-empty platters.

"Oh. Okay." Spencer didn't try to hide his disappointment. After Mom and Dad's disappearance, Uncle Mark had pulled Spencer out of school and brought him to Bearhaven for his own safety. Spencer hadn't exactly stayed put—he'd snuck onto the next bear rescue mission, determined to help—but since returning to Bearhaven, he'd been the only human here.

With Mom and Dad missing, Uncle Mark was the only family Spencer really had. They talked on video conference calls every night so they could at least see each other even though they weren't in the same place. Their calls always made Spencer miss his family a little bit less, and Uncle Mark usually gave Spencer an update on Mom and Dad. He'd been hoping for more good news from Uncle Mark tonight, and he'd wanted to tell his uncle about the progress he was making in STORM training.

But Uncle Mark also had an important role in Bearhaven. He had founded Bearhaven along with Mom and Dad and was a member of the Bear Council. Apparently, whatever the council was meeting about tonight was more important than talking to Spencer.

"Mi mi mi mi miii." Kate suddenly burst into her vocal warm-up, interrupting Spencer's thoughts. *Here we go again.* Spencer couldn't even count the number of times he'd heard Kate practice her twelve-word solo. He knew the cub was excited, but the concert wasn't for another few weeks!

"I'm going to my room," Spencer called to Lisle over the sounds of Kate's trilling. "I have to write in my STORM journal."

"All right," Lisle called back.

"I smell FLOWERS, dandelions, DAISIES, the sun is rising through the EVERGREEEEEENS," Kate sang.

Spencer slid off his seat and hurried into the living room. He grabbed his backpack and headed for the stairs. "Good night, Kate."

The cub waved a paw at Spencer. Her lungs were already filling with air to launch into another round of her solo.

3

The next morning, Spencer pushed his wooden plate across the table toward Aldo and Kate. The two bears suspiciously eyed what was left of Spencer's breakfast.

"Try it," he urged, licking a smear of Bearhaven Butter off his fingers. He had to admit, Raymond, Bearhaven's chef and the owner of Raymond's Cafe, had done a great job on his first attempt at making human-style peanut butter. Of course there were some other non-peanut kinds of nuts in the butter, and a few too many seeds Spencer didn't recognize, but for a first batch, this definitely satisfied Spencer's craving for his favorite food.

Aldo used his claw to pierce a slice of apple slathered with Bearhaven Butter. He popped it into his mouth. Kate looked on expectantly. Once it was clear Aldo wasn't going to spit out the apple, she reached for her own slice.

"Not bad," Aldo said as he smacked his lips. "It could use some honey, though."

Spencer laughed. Aldo was known for his sweet tooth. Kate ran her tongue over her teeth and opened and closed her mouth several times.

"Sticky!" she finally said.

"Sticky and delicious!" Spencer grabbed his STORM notebook from the table and stood up. "I have to give your dad my training update." He headed downstairs. Professor Weaver was probably waiting for Spencer now, ready to sign off on Spencer's STORM training progress before school.

The bottom floor of the Weavers' home was belowground and spread out around a honey-colored hallway. The big wooden door to Professor Weaver's study stood halfway open, its entrance framed by two beehive-shaped lights Bunny Weaver had designed. Bunny was Bearhaven's architect. She'd designed all the bears' homes and most of the other buildings in the hidden valley, but she'd also designed cool extra things for the Weavers' own house, like the beehive-shaped lights and massive dining room table.

Spencer was just about to knock on the door when Professor Weaver moved into view. Spencer froze. His hand hovered an inch from the wood. Usually Professor Weaver was a calm and patient bear. Spencer trusted him more than he trusted anyone else in Bearhaven. Today, though, Spencer could tell Professor Weaver was upset. His tan jowls were set in a firm line, and his blaze mark—the white triangular patch of fur on his chest—flashed in and out of Spencer's view as he paced back and forth.

"So we're back where we started then," Professor Weaver said.

"I'm afraid so." Uncle Mark's voice carried out of the room.

Uncle Mark?

Spencer let his hand fall to his side. He moved closer to the opening in the door to peek into the room.

Professor Weaver was still pacing back and forth, and Bunny was sitting back on her haunches looking up at a big screen. Two faces were projected on the screen: Uncle Mark's and his parents' assistant, Evarita. They were on a video conference call, just like the one Spencer and Uncle Mark were supposed to have had last night.

Uncle Mark ran a hand through his wavy blond hair. *Uh oh.* Whenever Uncle Mark ran his hand through his hair like that, it meant he was worried, and Uncle Mark was hardly ever worried. *Something must be wrong.* Spencer looked to Evarita's familiar face. She had dark circles under her eyes, as if she hadn't slept all night.

"I still don't understand," Bunny said. "We should have heard something by now. If Jane had any way of communicating . . ." Bunny's voice drifted off.

Spencer's entire body tensed. Jane was his mom, which meant that whatever was making Professor Weaver pace and Uncle Mark run his hand through his hair had to do with Mom and Dad. But what could Bunny mean? *If Jane had any way of communicating?* Professor Weaver said he got a message from Mom yesterday!

"I know, Bunny." Professor Weaver's voice was grim. "But we've been going over the details for hours now, and the situation is still the same: There hasn't been a single sign of the Plains in days. Things must have taken a turn for the worse. Unfortunately, we have no way of knowing what happened."

A turn for the worse? No sign of Mom and Dad in days? Spencer's heart started to pound. His mind was racing. He had to have heard the professor wrong. Just yesterday morning, Professor Weaver told him about a message from Mom. It said Mom and Dad were making their way back to Bearhaven. They were supposed to be arriving any day now.

Spencer wanted to scream and demand an explanation, but there was a huge lump rising in his throat. He didn't think any words would come out even if he could get his mouth to open.

"Well then, it isn't right, dear," Bunny replied. The BEAR-COM translated the tension in her voice. "The reports you've been giving Spencer—"

"Professor Weaver and I agreed together to give Spencer those reports," Uncle Mark interrupted. "We thought it would be better not to tell him that there's been no sign of Jane and Shane since the last mission. It's important that he doesn't lose hope right now." Evarita shook her head and looked away from the camera.

Spencer's stomach knotted. He could feel tears welling in his eyes. Uncle Mark and Professor Weaver had *lied* to him.

"They're his *parents*," Evarita said. "It's not right to keep the truth from him."

Tears started spilling down Spencer's cheeks. His teeth clenched. He was furious at Uncle Mark and Professor Weaver for lying to him, and terrified by what he was hearing. Nobody knew where Mom and Dad were, which could only mean they were in trouble. Big trouble.

"Spencer's just a cub. It's our responsibility to protect him," Professor Weaver stated, leaving no room for discussion. "We didn't tell him things have gotten worse because there's no use. He can't leave Bearhaven until his parents return. All he can do is stay here and wait. Scaring him with the truth won't change anything. And it won't get his parents back any faster."

Spencer had heard enough. He looked at the STORM training journal clutched in his left hand. He'd been gripping it so hard there was a deep crease in the cover. He shook his head angrily, trying to make the tears go away. What good would STORM training do him if he could never leave Bearhaven to use it? And who cared about rescuing bears when Mom and Dad were the ones who really needed saving? Spencer flung the journal on the floor and stormed off down the hall. He didn't want to be anywhere near Professor Weaver. The Weavers were supposed to be his family in Bearhaven. He'd even started to feel like they *were* his family.

The thought unleashed a new wave of anger. His *real* family was missing, and all the Weavers—and everybody else—had done was lie to him. Spencer's family wouldn't be arriving any day. That had all been part of the story he'd been told so he wouldn't fight having to stay in Bearhaven when Mom and Dad obviously needed help. Well, Spencer was done with being lied to. He was done with trusting the Weavers and Uncle Mark. And he was *really* done with being kept in Bearhaven when Mom and Dad needed help. His help.

4

"That took *forever!*" Kate said when Spencer arrived at the top of the stairs. She was still at the kitchen table, licking her bowl to catch any last drops of honey. "Was Dad happy you beat your river rescue record yesterday?"

Spencer swallowed hard, trying to get rid of the lump lodged in his throat. He nodded. Hopefully, Kate wouldn't see that his eyes were red and his nose was running. He swiped his hand across his face.

"Are you ready to go to school?" He was so angry at Professor Weaver and Uncle Mark, and so worried about Mom and Dad, he barely managed to get the sentence out. Kate didn't seem to notice. *Thank goodness.* Spencer needed time to make sense of everything he'd just overheard.

"Ready!" Kate slid off her seat. She trotted past Spencer and out the Weavers' front door. Spencer followed.

The bright morning sun made the moss-covered homes that stretched out in a row on either side of the Weavers' house look welcoming, but Spencer wasn't impressed anymore. He wasn't a guest in a cool valley filled with bears who invented amazing technology. He was a prisoner. He stomped down the Weavers' front path.

How was he supposed to sit in class and concentrate when he knew his parents were missing and in danger somewhere outside Bearhaven? And why should he even go to school? Doing what everyone told him to—going to school during the day, training with Aldo and Kate in the afternoon, waiting for news about his parents—wasn't getting him any closer to seeing Mom and Dad again. Did everyone expect him to just stay in Bearhaven forever? Actually, now Spencer knew that's *exactly* what they expected. "All he can do is stay here and wait," Professor Weaver had said.

"That's what they think," Spencer muttered.

Kate stopped walking and looked over her shoulder at Spencer. She eyed his legs suspiciously, as though something might be wrong with them. "Why are you walking so *slowly*?"

Spencer sped up. "I can't go to school today, Kate," he said once he'd reached her.

"But you have to." Kate frowned. "Mom and Dad and your uncle Mark all said you have to go to school with me."

"I know that!" Spencer snapped, and instantly felt bad. Kate was his best friend in Bearhaven. She'd never let him down. He needed her on his side, especially now that he knew nobody else was. "I'm sorry. It's just that I'm . . . I'm sort of upset about my parents still being missing, and I need some time to think."

"What do you need to think about?"

What I'm going to do to get them back myself, Spencer wanted to say, but he couldn't. If he said that then he'd have to explain everything to Kate, and he wasn't ready to repeat what he'd heard. Spencer just shrugged.

"Well, can't you think in school?" Kate's voice was hopeful.

Spencer shook his head. "Not with all the other cubs staring at me. They're not used to having me around. I feel like I'm a clown or something."

"You're just a new animal." Kate pawed at the ground. Spencer knew she loved bringing him to school. Her friendship with a human impressed the other cubs. But this was more important than showing him off. She had to understand.

"Will you help me, Kate? Will you cover for me?"

"How am I supposed to do that?" Kate huffed and started walking again.

"Tell them I'm sick! Tell them I'm not feeling well and had to go back to your house."

"What if I get in trouble?"

"You won't. I promise." *Please say yes.* When Kate didn't answer, Spencer tried pleading with her. "I'll do the dishes every night for a week." The cub kept walking. He dropped his voice to a whisper. "I'll wake up extra early this weekend and guard *Salmon King* so you can play instead of Winston and Jo-Jo." Kate's ears perked up a little bit at that. Winston and Jo-Jo *always* hogged *Salmon King*, especially on weekends. Still, she didn't answer. "Kate, *please*—" Before he could think of anything else to bargain with, a familiar cinnamon-colored ball of fur barreled out of a house on their left. It was Reggie, Kate's friend and one of Spencer's biggest fans in Bearhaven.

"Kate! Spencer!" Reggie raced toward them.

Not now, Reggie! Spencer stared at Kate, begging her with his eyes to agree to cover for him before Reggie caught up to them. Kate twitched her snout back and forth, like she was trying to sniff for the right answer, but hadn't found it yet.

"Hi!" Reggie scooted to a stop in front of them. "Spencer, check this out!" All of a sudden, the cub turned and ran back the way he came. He spun around to face Spencer and Kate, then rose onto his hind legs. He wobbled a little as he swung his paws out in front of him. "Bam!" Reggie yelled. He lurched forward, dropping back to all fours. He ran straight at Spencer and Kate, then jumped clumsily up into the air and tumbled to the ground in a disheveled summersault. His round, furry body flopped this way and that. Finally, he skidded to a halt on his belly at Spencer's feet, his front legs stretched out before him.

Spencer laughed despite his terrible morning and his determination to skip school. Reggie's performance—or *whatever* that was supposed to be—had been so unexpected Spencer couldn't help himself.

"What do you think?" Reggie asked. He was panting as he scrambled up to all fours.

"What do I think?" Spencer had no idea what Reggie was talking about.

"That was like stealing a base in baseball, right?"

"Oh," Spencer stifled his laughter. He didn't want to hurt Reggie's feelings. Yesterday, after school, Reggie had asked him all about his life at home. When Spencer told him about baseball, the cub had asked question after question until he'd heard every detail of how the game was played. Spencer must not have explained things as well as he'd thought. "Yeah, baseball is something like that," he finally said. The cub gave a happy shake.

"Should I show you again? You know, to remind you of your home?" Reggie turned to run off and give his "baseball" demonstration over again. At the word *home*, the lump returned to Spencer's throat. He shot Kate a look. *See?* There was no way Spencer could think in school, where almost every cub was as fascinated by him as Reggie was.

"Spencer's sick!" Kate blurted out.

"Are you okay?" Reggie whispered with concern. He turned back around and stepped up close to Spencer, searching him for signs of illness. "Do you need to go to Pinky's?"

"No," Spencer answered. He definitely didn't need to go to Pinky's Rehab Center and Salon. "It's just my stomach or something. I think I'll be fine after I lie down."

"He's going back to bed," Kate said. "But we should go to school before we're late." She motioned for Reggie to go ahead of her and lead the way down the path toward school. As soon as Reggie turned, she whispered to Spencer, "Dishes all week and *Salmon King* all weekend." Before Spencer could answer, she'd taken off at a run. "Feel better, Spencer!" she called over her shoulder.

5

Spencer stayed behind, at a safe distance, as he followed Kate and Reggie down the main path toward Bearhaven's center. The cubs took a left at Raymond's Cafe and trotted through the grassy clearing, past the flagpoles, and out toward the school building. Spencer cut off in a different direction.

He'd told Kate he wanted time to think, but that wasn't the whole truth. He'd been doing nothing but thinking, running through all the facts since he overheard the Weavers, Uncle Mark, and Evarita talking, and thinking wasn't making him feel any better. He needed to prove to himself that the Weavers and Uncle Mark couldn't keep him here, not when Mom and Dad were in danger. He wasn't their prisoner, and if he could show they were wrong about keeping him locked up in Bearhaven, maybe they would realize they were wrong about other things, too. Maybe he didn't need them to find Mom and Dad at all. Maybe he could find them himself. It was time Spencer took matters into his own hands. He'd start by breaking out of Bearhaven.

Spencer came to the base of a hill and started to climb. He found the path that led through the trees at the top of the hill to a clearing. The clearing held a hidden elevator that went two ways: either it rose up to a secret bridge above the trees, or it went down to Bearhaven's train, the TUBE. He'd taken this path two weeks before, when Uncle Mark and the team of bear operatives were leaving on the mission to rescue Ro Ro and her two cubs from Jay Grady's crummy carnival. Spencer had to sneak out of Bearhaven then to join the mission. But this time was different; now he needed to sneak out alone.

He stopped at the edge of the clearing. The huge tree that hid the elevator stood directly across from the path, but Spencer wouldn't be taking that route out of Bearhaven today. The minute the elevator started to move, the bear guard would know about it. Spencer eyed the long row of tightly packed trees that bordered the far side of the clearing. It was Bearhaven's outer wall, and it surrounded the entire valley. The trees created a natural barrier, keeping any unwanted visitors out. Squeezing between the rows and rows of closely planted trees would be impossible for any adult human. And *if* someone were able to get into the wall of trees, then they'd have the extra challenge of finding solid footing on the ground beneath them, which was a dangerous tangle of roots. Spencer knew it would be hard, but if he wanted to get out of Bearhaven without raising any alarms, finding a way through the wall of trees was his only option.

Spencer returned his attention to the clearing in front of him. There was no one in sight, but the bears' security had positioned surveillance cameras everywhere. If Spencer stepped into the clearing right now, his image would appear on a screen in front of whichever Bear Guard member was on duty.

Spencer looked up into the trees. He didn't see any cameras, but he didn't think the bears would have been that obvious anyway. They were much more sophisticated. There was no way B.D., the head of Bearhaven security, would have left a camera out in plain sight where anyone could see it. Spencer scanned the big sturdy limbs. There were just leaves, a beehive, a bird's nest . . .

Wait! The beehive was so perfectly shaped it had to be fake, just like the lights in the Weavers' house Bunny had designed. Spencer crept up to the tree.

He grabbed a pebble from the ground. *Might as well double check to make sure it's not real.* Climbing a tree only to be attacked by a swarm of real bees didn't seem like the best idea. Taking aim, Spencer threw the pebble at the beehive. It hit its mark, but nothing happened. There wasn't so much as a buzz. *Definitely fake. Definitely a camera.*

Spencer wished the Bear Guard hid their cameras in low bushes instead of trees he had to climb. He *hated* climbing, no matter how high. He dreaded the moment his feet left the ground, but if he wanted to leave Bearhaven without getting caught, this was the only way. Somehow, he had to stop the beehive surveillance camera from filming him. He wrapped his arms around the tree trunk.

"It's just like STORM training," Spencer whispered, trying to reassure himself. "Let your legs do most of the work," was the first pointer Aldo had given him. But when that tactic hadn't helped Spencer get himself off the ground, Aldo had tried another approach that *was* working during Spencer's training sessions. Aldo said: "Just pretend you're a bear."

Taking a deep breath, Spencer shimmied up onto one of the lowest branches. Climbing a little higher, he crouched down and lowered his belly onto a branch, then slid forward until he was stretched out over the beehive. *Don't look down.* The worst thing about climbing was the possibility of falling . . .

Not now. Spencer focused on the camera. He didn't want to cause any damage to Bearhaven's security equipment. Professor Weaver made all of the bears' cool technology, and no matter how angry Spencer was with the professor, breaking the camera would be going too far. Instead, Spencer reached down and untied his left shoelace, then removed the lace from the shoe altogether.

Grabbing a skinny, leafy branch nearby, Spencer snapped it off the tree. He used the shoelace as a length of rope and tied a figure eight knot around the end of the small branch, just the way Dad had taught him. He tied the free end of the shoelace around the branch beneath him.

"Here goes nothing," he muttered and released his leafy shield so that it dropped into position in front of the beehive. Hopefully, in the Bear Guard's surveillance room, it would look as if a branch had accidentally fallen in front of the camera's lens.

Spencer inched backward on the branch and climbed down to the ground as quickly as he could with the unlaced sneaker slipping around on his foot. He ran to the opposite side of the clearing, approaching the wall of tightly packed trees. He slipped between two trunks and was immediately faced with another tree blocking his way. He slipped past it, and again faced two more. He looked for another opening.

With lots of squeezing and stumbling over roots, Spencer made his way deep into the wall of trees.

By the time Spencer stood sandwiched between two trees on the outer edge of the wall, his T-shirt was dirty and his arms were scraped from twisting and squeezing past so much rough bark. Getting through Bearhaven's outer wall had been harder than he'd expected, but his anger at Professor Weaver and Uncle Mark for lying to him hadn't faded a bit. Each time Spencer considered turning back, he'd heard Professor Weaver's voice in his head, *All he can do is stay here and wait.* It made Spencer even more determined to get outside Bearhaven's walls.

"I can do a lot more than stay in Bearhaven and wait," he whispered to himself. And he was in the middle of proving it. Spencer wasn't going to be anyone's prisoner. He could leave Bearhaven whenever he wanted.

Crack!

Spencer jumped at the sound of a branch snapping above him. There was a quick rustling of leaves. He looked up. Hundreds of branches were woven together to create a thick canopy, so it was impossible to see through them from above: another layer of Bearhaven's cool security.

Hopefully, that's a bird, or the wind . . . Spencer couldn't get caught now, not after he'd made it this far. As soon as he pushed himself through this last small gap in the wall of trees, he'd be out of Bearhaven's territory.

Spencer scanned the forest, searching for a surveillance camera. He didn't see another beehive anywhere. This spot in the perimeter of Bearhaven seemed clear of cameras, but Spencer had a good reason for double checking: He had gotten a glimpse of the bears' surveillance once before—and he knew how sophisticated it was.

On his first visit to the Lab, one of their surveillance screens had shown a girl in the woods right outside this very same wall of trees. B.D., the Head of the Bear Guard, had said she was a security concern, but he wouldn't tell Spencer anything else about her. Spencer had overheard B.D. talking and he learned the girl's name was Kirby. He calculated that when the security camera caught Kirby on tape, she couldn't have been far from where Spencer was standing now. Still, he couldn't find a beehive anywhere. He'd have to trust that this part of the perimeter wasn't under surveillance.

Spencer shimmied sideways and stepped out of Bearhaven's tree wall, leaving the bears' territory. He was free! He could go anywhere. But he didn't really have anywhere to go. With Mom and Dad missing, it wasn't safe for Spencer to go home. Even if he could, he wouldn't know how to get there. He wanted to look for his parents, but without any leads on Mom and Dad's location, he'd never know where to even start the search.

Spencer kicked a pebble. Maybe leaving Bearhaven was a mistake. It *did* make him feel a little better to know he could leave the bears' community when he wanted to. But so what? He couldn't exactly tell the Weavers or anyone else in Bearhaven he had left without getting in a lot of trouble. Even though he knew he wouldn't be able to use this escape to prove anything, Spencer didn't want to turn back just yet. It was the first time in a week he'd been outside the bears' valley. Besides, what good was all of his STORM training going to do him if he never got to test it in the outside world?

That's it! Spencer had the perfect explanation for why he had left Bearhaven: He needed to get some real world STORM training. He could tell the Weavers he needed to put his skills to the test. He couldn't get in trouble for being dedicated to his training . . . could he?

Not if I actually train, Spencer thought. He grabbed two nearby sticks and crossed them in an *X* on the ground to mark the spot on Bearhaven's perimeter he'd need to return to.

Satisfied he'd be able to find his way back, Spencer set out into the woods in front of him. He went into operative mode, putting silent walking, one of his Stealth skills from STORM training, into action right away. Rather than crunch through the woods, he walked using all the muscles in his body, quieting each of his steps. He and Kate had practiced this a lot. It was hard with one shoelace missing; his left sneaker kept slipping off and flopping down onto the leaves, making a smacking sound. Soon though, Spencer got into the rhythm of it. He crept through the forest, continuing deeper into the woods.

Something rustled nearby. Spencer spun around. It sounded too small to be a bear, but Spencer couldn't shake the feeling of somebody following him.

"Dangit!" At the sight of a tiny red light, he ducked behind the closest tree. *Bearhaven has security cameras all the way out here?* He poked his head out from behind the tree. There it was. The red light he'd just spotted was nestled in the branches of a birch tree. Spencer didn't see a beehive. *Why would they conceal the cameras near Bearhaven, but not out here? Unless the camera didn't belong to Bearhaven . . .*

Spencer crept from tree to tree until he was standing behind the birch. The camera was low enough that he could see it without climbing, but the fact that it wasn't high in the tree wasn't the only suspicious detail Spencer noticed. Whoever had put the camera in the tree had tried to camouflage it, painting it green, brown, and black. But, even with the paint, Spencer could tell the camera wasn't high-tech or surveillance-worthy at all. It looked just like the old video camera Dad toted around to all of Spencer's T-ball games when he was little. This camera wasn't one of Bearhaven's. But who else could be watching the forest?

Suddenly, Spencer heard footsteps behind him. Then a voice.

"Freeze."

6

Spencer spun around.

"Hey!"

"Hey!" Spencer yelled back, shocked by who he found behind him. He recognized her immediately. It was Kirby, the girl who B.D. had been watching on Bearhaven's surveillance cameras two weeks ago.

"I told you to freeze!" Kirby was wearing a green backpack slung over one shoulder with a few black cables poking out of its front pocket. The camera was definitely hers. The paint camouflaging the camera matched a streak of paint on one of her bag's shoulder straps. Maybe B.D. was right to keep an eye on this girl.

"Sorry," Spencer mumbled. He was too busy looking Kirby over to take her orders too seriously. She looked as if she might be a little older than he was, but not much. The big sunglasses blocking her face made it hard to tell. Spencer stared at the sunglasses. Something about them seemed funny, plus, it was weird she was wearing sunglasses at all. There wasn't any sun shining in the heavily shaded woods. There was a rustling in the trees nearby and Kirby jumped. When she whipped her head around to look, Spencer realized why the glasses looked so strange. Cheng, one of Spencer's best friends from home, had a pair just like them. They were spy glasses with extra wide lenses to make room for little mirrors. Whoever was wearing them could see behind themselves. Cheng said it was like having eyes in the back of his head.

"Cool glasses," he said. "My friend has a pair of those."

Kirby returned her attention to Spencer.

"Want to try them on?" Before Spencer could answer, Kirby pulled off the sunglasses and handed them to him.

Spencer took the glasses, surprised by how willing Kirby was to share the cool gear. A minute ago he'd thought she was going to attack him for taking a look at the camera she'd rigged in a tree. Now she was handing him her stuff to try on?

"Hey, what's your name anyway?" Kirby asked.

"Spencer."

"I'm Kirby."

I know, Spencer wanted to answer.

Kirby was already moving on to question him.

"What are you doing here?" she asked. "Hikers don't usually come this far out."

Spencer slipped on the sunglasses, stalling as his mind raced to come up with an excuse. "I'm a Boy Scout," he said finally, still thinking of Cheng. Cheng talked about his Boy Scout troop all the time. If Spencer could remember enough of what his friend had said, he might just get away with the lie. "My troop's out here." He gestured casually around the woods.

"And you got lost?" Kirby scanned the woods as though searching for more Boy Scouts. When she returned her gaze to Spencer, he was suddenly very aware that the Cougars

T-shirt and jeans he was wearing looked nothing like a Boy Scout uniform.

"No, it's . . . we're doing our survival challenges, so we have to go out alone and . . . survive."

Kirby cocked her head to one side and looked Spencer over, as though deciding whether or not to accept his story. Her eyes landed on his laceless sneaker. "What happened to your shoe lace?"

"Oh, I used it to tie up my food, in a tree. To keep it away from . . ." Spencer hesitated. He was afraid that even saying the word would give something away.

"Bears?" Kirby said it for him.

"Yeah, bears," Spencer mumbled.

"Have you seen one?!" Kirby exclaimed, her eyes wide with excitement. "I caught one on camera a few weeks ago!" She crossed her arms. "There's something going on with bears in these woods. Their tracks are everywhere. I spend more time here than anyone, so I would know."

"So you live around here?" Spencer looked around. If Kirby lived here, it definitely didn't seem like she had any neighbors. Nobody in Bearhaven had mentioned any humans other than Kirby living in these woods.

"I do everything around here," Kirby answered.

Before Spencer could ask what that was supposed to mean, he was distracted by a flash of movement in the little mirrors at the corners of the spy glasses. Spencer's eyes locked on the mirrors, searching the woods behind him. Something—or someone—was slowly moving through the trees toward them.

7

Spencer looked over his shoulder, trying to act casual. Were the mirrored glasses playing tricks on him? He was sure he'd seen something moving through the woods, but there was no sign of it now.

"I'll take those back," Kirby said suddenly, holding out a hand for the spy glasses. Spencer slid them off.

"They're really cool." He handed the glasses over. "So what else do you have set up out here? Aside from that camera." Spencer nodded to the camouflage-painted camera in the tree.

"I have two of those cameras," Kirby answered, straightening up. "They record onto memory cards, then I collect the cards and watch them for anything out of the ordinary. I also have a hidden microphone and three controlled locations throughout the forest—"

"Controlled locations?" Spencer interrupted. That sounded important.

"Right. So they're like this." Kirby grabbed a stick from the ground and drew a big circle in the dirt around herself and Spencer. "Three sections of dirt clear enough for me to study. One on the hiking trail and two deeper into the

37

woods. I check on them every day, looking for bear tracks or other unusual details."

Spencer looked around the circle Kirby had drawn. Hopefully, Kirby's controlled locations weren't anywhere too close to Bearhaven's outer wall . . . With all her equipment and studying of the woods, she might actually be able to discover something Bearhaven's bears wouldn't want her to know. Especially if she really checked her surveillance systems every single day.

"Your parents let you walk around in here alone? Whenever you want?" he asked.

"My parents work a lot." She shrugged, fiddling with the compass hooked to her backpack. She hadn't exactly answered the question, but Spencer understood. After all, Mom and Dad worked a lot, too. But it didn't sound as though Kirby had someone like Evarita watching her when her parents weren't around.

Maybe all of Kirby's freedom wasn't as cool as it sounded. Even when Spencer was in Bearhaven he had Kate to hang out with, and at home he had his human friends. No wonder Kirby spent so much time watching the woods for suspicious activity, and no wonder she was so eager to tell him about it. She didn't have anyone to talk to.

Spencer turned back to the camera in the birch tree. He put a hand on it, hoping to pull it down and take a better look.

"Hey! Don't do that!" Kirby launched herself at Spencer, knocking his hand away from the camera. Spencer stumbled backward he was so surprised.

Just then, a bear crashed through the trees and hurtled toward them.

"AHHHH!" Kirby shrieked. *No!* Spencer saw with horror a flash of pink at the bear's neck. He rushed forward, grabbing Kirby by the arm. He pushed her behind the birch tree as quickly as he could. "Stay here!" he yelled, then jumped out to face Kate, screaming at the top of his lungs.

Kate was crouching on the other side of the birch, snarling at the trees. She looked ready to tackle anyone who stepped out from behind it. *She's protecting me!* Spencer realized. *She thinks Kirby is trying to hurt me!* Kate tried to move between him and the birch as though to shield him from another attack, but Spencer sidestepped her. If he didn't act fast, Kirby would peek out from behind the tree and see Kate and her sparkly, pink BEAR-COM.

"Ahhh!" he yelled. "Get out of here!" He glared at Kate urgently. "Go!" Kate's mouth dropped open. Confusion flashed in her eyes. *This is for her own good,* Spencer told himself as he yelled at her again. She may have thought she was protecting him, but now he had to protect *her* and all of Bearhaven from being discovered. Didn't she know she was wearing her BEAR-COM? If Kirby saw it, there was no telling what she'd figure out! *Kate will understand later.* "Shoo! Don't bother us! Go away!"

Kate shuffled backward, her eyes locked on Spencer's. He could tell he was scaring her. "I SAID GO!!"

Kate let out a small whimper, then turned and ran back into the trees. Spencer watched her crash away until she'd gone so far he lost sight of her. *I'm sorry, Kate!* he wanted to yell. Her feelings were definitely hurt. He wished he could run after her and explain, but right now he had to make sure Kirby hadn't seen the BEAR-COM. If she was already onto Bearhaven's bears, letting information fall into her hands about the BEAR-COM was just too dangerous. He felt horrible about how he'd treated Kate. But there would be time to fix things with her later.

8

"That was crazy!" Kirby whispered, poking her head out from behind the birch tree.

"Yeah, the bear really came out of nowhere," Spencer said carefully. "Luckily, I think it was just a cub."

"Luckily?" Kirby gasped. "Don't they teach you *anything* in Boy Scouts? If there's a cub, there's probably a mother bear nearby, and everybody knows that mother bears are *fierce* when it comes to protecting their cubs. As soon as I get photos of the bear prints, we should get out of here."

"Oh. I don't think . . . I don't get the feeling there's a mother bear around here. We should be okay." Spencer suddenly realized it wasn't just Kirby who might have seen Kate's BEAR-COM. He cast a sideways glance in the camera's direction. What if it had caught everything on film?

"What do you mean, you don't get the *feeling*?" Kirby followed Spencer's eyes. A second later she stepped out from behind the tree. She glared at Spencer. "You knocked my camera over when you tried to grab it!" She yelled. "Look! It's pointing up into the tree! The footage will be of leaves, and that's not going to do me any good! Not when there was a real bear *right* here."

"You knocked my hand against the camera when you attacked me!" Spencer shot back.

Kirby stomped over to the tree and retrieved the camera. Spencer held his breath. It seemed too good to be true. Kirby fiddled with the camera. She groaned, confirming that she hadn't recorded Kate. "I would've gotten video of that cub if it wasn't for you."

"You would've been *eaten* by that cub if it wasn't for me!" Spencer tried to sound defensive, but really, he wanted to cheer. He'd saved Kate from being caught on film!

"Bears don't eat humans," Kirby muttered. She popped the card out of the camera and replaced it with one she fished out of her backpack.

"How many of those cards do you have anyway?" Spencer asked, hoping to distract Kirby from her frustration. It worked.

"Just four," Kirby answered. "A card for each of my two cameras to record on, then a replacement for when they get full. If I find anything suspicious on them, I record *that* footage onto my computer. Then I swap them with the cards in the cameras and record over the old footage."

Spencer decided he liked Kirby. Her surveillance was pretty cool, even if it did give B.D. and the rest of the Bear Guard headaches. For a second, Spencer wished he could tell Kirby about the Bear Guard and how they were trained to watch her carefully. It was the best compliment he could give her for all her surveillance systems. She was good enough to be monitored.

"There's something going on in these woods," Kirby said, reminding Spencer exactly why he couldn't mention the Bear

Guard. Kirby replaced the camera in the crook of the birch. "And I'm not going to stop until I find out what it is."

Spencer looked down at his dirty sneakers. Kirby seemed determined to solve the mystery of the woods. Even though that was bad news for Bearhaven, Spencer knew how she felt. He was trying to do the same thing—get to the bottom of his parents' disappearance—and he wasn't going to stop at anything, either.

"I could show you the rest," Kirby said, interrupting Spencer's thoughts.

"The rest?"

"I mean my microphone, and the other cameras and stuff." Kirby's voice was hopeful, as if she was desperate for the chance to finally share her cool surveillance with someone.

"Actually, I should get going," Spencer said a little guiltily. He was pretty sure he was the first kid Kirby had seen in a long time. And it might be a long time before she saw another one. But he really had to get back to Bearhaven before he got himself and Kate into trouble . . . and he definitely needed to apologize to Kate right away.

"But you can't go yet!" Kirby practically shouted. "That cub's probably still around here somewhere. Or worse, its mother. We should stick together until we're absolutely certain the coast is clear."

"Oh," Spencer hesitated. "Don't worry, I think the coast is clear. Uh . . . it was nice to meet you, though."

"Wait a minute." Kirby pulled a pen and a notebook out of the depths of her green backpack. She started scrawling on a blank page. "If you see anything suspicious while you're in the forest—any clues, or any more bears, or anything fishy at all—come find me. I'll need a full report, all right? You owe me. Don't forget."

"I owe *you*?"

Kirby didn't look up from her notebook, she just jerked her head in the direction of her camera as she tore out the sheet of paper. Spencer sighed.

"These are the coordinates of my house."

Spencer examined the list of numbers. *Can real Boy Scouts read this stuff?* "Okay, got it," he said, folding the paper and stuffing it into his pocket. "Now I know where to find you."

9

Spencer made his way back to Bearhaven's outer wall. When he arrived at the barrier of trees marking the perimeter of the bears' territory, he followed it until he found the *X* he'd made to mark the spot he'd emerged from. He tossed the two sticks aside and glanced over his shoulder, checking for the millionth time that Kirby hadn't followed him. She hadn't.

Spencer reached into his pocket for the black jade bear figurine and let it rest in his open palm. The bear figurine had been a gift from Mom and Dad on Spencer's eighth birthday. He kept it with him as a reminder that, like a bear, he could be strong, smart, and brave. No matter how far away Mom and Dad were, it always made Spencer feel closer to them to look at the jade bear.

"This doesn't mean I'm giving up," Spencer whispered. He wasn't going to leave Bearhaven to find Mom and Dad today, but at least now he knew he could when he needed to. He slipped the jade bear back into his pocket.

Spencer turned sideways and squeezed between a pair of trees. Returning to the bears' territory was just as difficult as leaving, but after what felt like hours of twisting and turning, he stepped out into the clearing in Bearhaven.

"Darn," he muttered. Kate wasn't there waiting for him like he'd hoped. *I wouldn't be waiting for me, either.* Spencer could imagine how confused and hurt Kate must be. She'd jumped out to protect him from Kirby, and he'd turned around and protected Kirby from Kate. At least, that's how it must have looked to the cub.

He wished he hadn't been so mean to Kate or sounded so angry . . . but what was he supposed to do? If he hadn't scared her away, Kirby would definitely have seen Kate's pink BEAR-COM. There was no telling how many of Kirby's clues might connect! And how much Kirby might learn about Bearhaven.

Spencer brushed himself off and jogged across the clearing toward the beehive he had tampered with hours earlier. The shield of leaves he'd rigged with his shoelace was still intact, blocking the view of the Bear Guard's surveillance camera. *I've already climbed this tree today,* he thought, approaching the one he'd need to climb. *Just remember what Aldo said: "Pretend you're a bear."* Spencer scrambled up into the tree.

He crept out onto one of the branches and looked down past the beehive to the ground below. It wasn't far, but Spencer's heart started to race. He took a deep breath and focused on the beehive. He moved as quickly as he could to untie the shoelace and let the bundle of leaves fall away from the camera, but it wasn't fast enough. The panic that always seemed to overcome him when he was high off the ground hit him suddenly. Familiar images Spencer couldn't explain filled his head: metal, blood, a bear's face only inches from his own, leaves and branches snapping against him as he fell. The images always felt like pieces of a nightmare, or a bad memory, but Spencer had no idea where they came from, or why they made his whole body freeze up in fear. He gulped, his heart racing, and gripped the branch below him as hard as he could. After a second, Spencer managed to push the horrible feeling away. He returned to the ground to relace his sneaker.

Now he just had to find Kate. Spencer took off down the path toward the center of town. He'd start at the Weavers'.

When Spencer stepped through the Weavers' front door, he found Bunny sitting on one of the oversized couches in the living room, her back turned to him. She didn't move to greet him. *Does she already know I skipped school? Is she mad that Kate covered for me?* He couldn't imagine Bunny really getting angry at him, but even disappointment from the usually caring mother bear would be hard to take.

Bunny let out a quiet snore. *She's napping!* Spencer silent-walked through the living room and stole down the stairs. He raced down the hall to the room Kate shared with Lisle. He pressed his ear against the door, but he didn't hear anything. He pushed it open and crept into the dark room.

"Kate?" he whispered as his eyes adjusted.

Unlike most of the other rooms in the Weavers' house, Lisle and Kate's room didn't have any furniture in it, since the bears' bedrooms were meant to feel the most den-like. Two nooks were carved into the small room's walls, one for Lisle and one for Kate. In each nook there was a lumpy layer of cushioning for a bear to curl up on.

The room was empty.

Spencer went to his own room and poked his head in. Even after two weeks in Bearhaven, his bedroom at the Weavers' was still a happy surprise. It was identical to his room at home. Everything from the curtains in the windows to the books on the bookshelf was the same. Mom had copied his bedroom perfectly, just so when he was here, in Bearhaven, it was one thing he wouldn't have to miss. The room looked as familiar as ever, but right now Spencer didn't want to pretend this was really his bedroom at home. He wanted a bear cub—namely Kate Weaver—to be waiting for him inside.

She wasn't. Spencer dropped to his hands and knees to check under his bunk bed just in case. Kate had slept under there to keep him company his first night in Bearhaven. But now, no Kate.

Spencer checked every possible hiding spot in the Weavers' family room, then he looked under their enormous dining room table. Kate wasn't here, either. He started to climb the stairs to the Weavers' living room.

Bunny's voice stopped him short. "You mean to say they never went to school? . . . Neither of them?"

Spencer heard an answer come through Bunny's BEAR-COM, but he was too far away to make out the words. "All right, Mr. Bee. Thank you for letting me know . . . Yes, of course." Spencer listened to the creaking of the couch as Bunny stood up, then the soft padding of her paws on the floor as she moved around the room. After a second, the front door thumped shut. The house fell silent around him.

I have to find Kate before Bunny does, or we're both going to be in a whole lot of trouble.

10

Spencer stomped down the empty dock. The sun was setting, and his determination to apologize to Kate was starting to fade. He was getting frustrated with her now. Why was she still hiding? Now they were both going to get in trouble! Where *was* she?

A cinnamon-brown head splashed to the surface of the river. "Well, it's not like she can *fly*," Reggie said, rolling himself up onto the dock. "She doesn't have *wings*." He chuckled, then gave himself a tremendous, full-body shake, soaking Spencer in river water. "She's just a better hider than I thought, I guess."

Spencer sighed. When he'd first run into Reggie on his way out of the Weavers' house, he'd thought the cub might be helpful in his search for Kate. After all, Reggie would know all of Kate's favorite places. He might even know some hiding spots around Bearhaven Spencer hadn't found out about yet.

At first, he'd been right. Reggie had taken Spencer to investigate a secret dugout some of the cubs had made near Raymond's Café's vegetable garden. Joanne, the bear who managed all the gardens, had been there, turning soil with her claws, but not Kate. Then they'd checked the school, because Reggie thought Kate might be sorry about skipping out. "Maybe she went to apologize to Professor Spady for missing class," the cub had said gravely. "That's what I would do. Professor Spady is *really* strict about that stuff."

After hiding behind a boulder in the schoolyard only to have Reggie return from Professor Spady's classroom without Kate, Spencer decided to go back to his original plan of checking the dock. He'd tried to leave Reggie then, but the cub wasn't so easy to lose.

"She's got to be around here somewhere," Spencer muttered, wiping water droplets off his face. "Right?" The rotten feeling in Spencer's stomach suddenly got a whole lot worse. *What if Kate hasn't come back to Bearhaven yet? What if she didn't make it back at all?*

"KATE!" Reggie suddenly bellowed, startling Spencer so much he nearly fell into the river. "KATE!"

"What are you doing? Why are you yelling like that?"

The cub shrugged. "It's almost my dinnertime. I thought if she knew we were looking for her, this might go faster."

Dinnertime! Kate would never miss dinner! None of the bears would! Spencer took off running.

"Hey! Where are you going?" Reggie followed him down the dock.

"I'm going to the Weavers'! You're right, Reggie! She'll be back for dinner!"

She has to be . . .

Reggie didn't answer but raced alongside Spencer until they turned down the path to the Weavers' house. "See you later!" the cub called, peeling off. "Tell Kate she's a great hider. I'm *definitely* on her team next time we play Hide-and-Go-Hunt!"

Spencer waved and slowed down. Professor Weaver was up ahead, pushing open the door of his house. *Great.* Spencer let the huge bear enter, then he counted to ten and approached. Sneaking in probably wasn't an option—the bears usually smelled him long before he entered a room—but it was worth a shot.

Spencer crept up the Weavers' front path. He put both hands on the big wooden door and quietly eased it open.

"Spencer?" Bunny shrilled before he'd even set foot inside.

Spencer swung the door open the rest of the way. Inside stood Bunny, Professor Weaver, Winston, and Jo-Jo. They all stared at him. No Kate.

"Come on inside, son," Professor Weaver said. "Sounds like you have some explaining to do." *YOU have some explaining to do, too!* Spencer wanted to reply, but now wasn't the time.

"I'd say so!" Bunny growled. *Uh-oh.* Spencer gulped and stepped into the living room. He was definitely in trouble. Bunny didn't offer him so much as a reassuring smile. She padded urgently over to the open doorway to search the path outside. "Spencer, where's Kate? Isn't she with you?"

"Told you she wasn't with him," Winston grumbled.

"She'll show up for dinner, Mom. What're we having anyway?" Jo-Jo sniffed toward the kitchen.

"Hush, boys," Bunny snapped. She slammed the front door shut. "Did you not skip school *together*, Spencer?"

Spencer shook his head. His stomach twisted and flopped. "I haven't seen her since this morning."

51

"I don't understand," Bunny said. "If she wasn't with you, then where is she? She's never skipped school before. She loves school. This wasn't your idea, then? I was sure—"

"Bunny, please try to remain calm," Professor Weaver interrupted.

Bunny started to pace. "Winston and Jo-Jo have been looking for her since school got out. Kate knows it's nearly dinnertime. If she's not here by now . . . I just can't imagine . . . I think we ought to call B.D."

"There's no need to panic, dear. We can't call the Head of the Bear Guard just because our cub has decided to play a little game of Hide-and-Go-Hunt. I'll call Aldo." Professor Weaver lifted a claw to his BEAR-COM, preparing to radio his oldest son. "There's only so much trouble a cub can get into in Bearhaven."

Spencer's heart began to pound. The rotten feeling in his stomach got so bad he thought he might throw up right there in the Weavers' living room. What if Kate wasn't *in* Bearhaven? What if something was really wrong? What if she was in danger? His mind raced. He had to tell them what he knew. Bunny was going to kill him! This was all his fault! But if Kate needed help . . .

"She might not be in Bearhaven!" he blurted out.

Bunny, who had been pacing back and forth, whipped around to face him. A snarl formed on her lips. Winston and Jo-Jo's eyes widened as they watched their father rise up onto his hind legs. Professor Weaver stared gravely down at Spencer from his full, looming height.

"Spencer Plain, *what* are you talking about?" Bunny let out a low, terrifying growl.

11

Spencer's palm was sweating around the jade bear in his pocket. Bunny had been reprimanding him in a thundering growl for the last five minutes. He'd confessed to the Weavers that Kate had followed him out of Bearhaven, and then he'd scared her off into the woods. Once he'd finished speaking, Bunny unleashed her mother bear fury, huffing and popping her jaw as she growled her disbelief that Spencer could have done something so careless. Now her fierce scolding seemed to be coming to an end at last, but Spencer had a bad feeling things were about to get a whole lot worse.

"*Anything* could happen to her out there," Bunny finished, her voice dropping to a threatening growl. She turned away from Spencer, who had a lump in his throat the size of a baseball. He could barely keep himself from running back out of Bearhaven right now to search the woods for Kate himself.

Professor Weaver loomed over Spencer. Without saying a word, he lifted a claw to his BEAR-COM and activated an alarm, calling all Bear Council members for an emergency meeting. Then he turned and left the house.

Bunny's BEAR-COM suddenly flashed yellow, receiving the alarm Professor Weaver had activated. It began repeating the emergency message that called her and all the other members of the Bear Council to "Report immediately." She snarled and shut it off. Rushing to the door, she growled to Winston and Jo-Jo in Ragayo, then left the house. The door banged shut behind her.

"This is all my fault," Spencer groaned. He slumped onto one of the Weavers' couches. What if Kate was hurt? Or lost? Or worse?

He didn't get very far in imagining where Kate could be or what might have happened to her. Five minutes later the Weavers' front door swung open again. It was Aldo.

"I'm supposed to bring you to the Lab," the bear announced in a flat voice. His eyes searched Spencer's face as though trying to find some reasonable explanation for why his little sister was missing and possibly in danger.

"I'm sorry, Aldo," Spencer said, his voice wavering. "I'll do anything I can to help find her."

Aldo shook his head. "I'm not going to be the only bear to say this to you tonight, Spencer, but I think you've done enough. Let's go." With that, Aldo turned and started back down the path. He didn't check to see if Spencer was following.

"Aldo, I promise, it was all a big mistake." Spencer rushed to catch up with the bear.

"I know," Aldo said. "But she's only a cub, and if she's lost in the woods somewhere, there's no telling . . ." The bear fixed Spencer with a serious stare. "We just have to find her, that's all."

Spencer followed Aldo out into the darkening valley. The lanterns that illuminated Bearhaven when the sun went down were just being lit. A poster for the Weaver Family Singers concert was tacked to one of the lantern posts. Spencer looked away as they passed. Out of the corner of his eye, he saw Aldo do the same. *Kate's not missing that concert. No matter what,* Spencer promised himself.

He and Aldo reached the riverbank and stepped through a row of trees nearby. Soon, the Lab came into view. It was still the coolest building Spencer had ever seen. The Lab was made of a gleaming, pitted metal. It was shaped like a dome and it didn't have a single door or window. Instead, anyone who was authorized to enter could breathe on the Lab's outer wall, and the wall would open in response to their breath. The bears on the guard and the council were the only ones who were supposed to know how it worked, but Aldo had accidentally explained it to Spencer once. The Lab was made of a special metal that responded to the DNA in the breath of whoever was trying to get in.

Aldo approached the building. He leaned forward and breathed on the metal wall. The metal rippled and retracted, then disappeared, opening a hole large enough to step through.

"Are you coming with me?" Spencer asked.

"I think I'd better. Mom's dangerous right now."

Aldo was right, Bunny *was* dangerous. Just like Kirby said, mother bears were the most threatening when they were protecting their young. They could act ferociously if they thought their cub was in harm's way. Spencer wondered what Mom would do if he went missing. Would she be as fierce and protective and dangerous as Bunny? He hoped so.

"I can't imagine the council is going to be very friendly to you, either," Aldo went on. "Besides, it's my sister . . . I want to know what's going on, too." Aldo nodded for Spencer to lead the way. A second after they stepped through, the wall sealed shut behind them.

"Let's get this over with," Spencer whispered. He understood why Bunny was so mad. After all, his own anger about *his* family being in danger was what had gotten them all into this mess. But facing Bunny again definitely wasn't something he was looking forward to.

Spencer followed Aldo down the sleek white corridor to the Bear Guard's surveillance room. B.D. and Professor Weaver were there, leaning toward the large bank of computer screens. The images on the screens were live video feeds from all the security cameras hidden around Bearhaven. Professor Weaver and B.D. were staring at one in particular. A bear Spencer didn't recognize was cowering behind them. He wore silver cuffs on his two front legs, marking him as a member of the Bear Guard, just like Aldo and B.D. From the way the silver cuffs gleamed with no scratches or marks, Spencer figured he was probably just as new to the guard as Aldo.

"Why didn't you say something when the camera view was obstructed?" B.D. grumbled. He rewound the footage on one of the cameras, then squinted as it played back.

"I don't know . . . I just . . . they were just leaves," the bear stammered.

Spencer looked past the bears to the video screen, which was filled with leaves. It was impossible to see anything beyond them. He swallowed hard. He hadn't thought covering the camera would do any harm. Now he realized how wrong he'd been.

"There!" Professor Weaver shouted. He pointed a claw at the screen. "I saw a shadow, just there. Can you make it out? Is it Kate?" The hopefulness in the professor's voice made Spencer's stomach flop for the millionth time.

"Spencer's here, Dad," Aldo said into the grim silence that fell in the room.

Professor Weaver didn't take his eyes off the leafy footage, but B.D. turned to face Spencer. "Let's go," the enormous jet-black Head of the Guard said gruffly. The furless patch at his jaw rippled as he spoke. He marched over to a silver platform at the far side of the room. Spencer and Aldo followed. "You can go, Aldo. I'll take Spencer from here," B.D. added. But when he turned around, Aldo was still following behind them.

"I was hoping—" Aldo started.

"You know council meetings are closed." B.D. cut him off. "Stay here. Keep watching the cameras and searching the surveillance videos. You'll need to take Spencer home once we've heard what he has to say." Spencer's heart started to beat a little faster. He didn't want to face Bunny and the rest of the council alone.

Aldo nodded. His orders were clear. He shuffled back a few paces, away from the silver platform. "Good luck, little man," he said to Spencer. "Tell them everything you can."

"Thanks," Spencer whispered. He could feel B.D.'s eyes boring down on him.

B.D.'s claw hovered over the white button hidden on the wall beside them. "Professor, are you coming?"

"I'll be along in just a minute," Professor Weaver answered. He continued to search the screen.

B.D. pressed the white button. *Whoosh!* Spencer felt himself begin to sink as the platform dropped from the Bear Guard's surveillance room down to the secret corridor below. For a moment, everything was dark, then the platform came to a hydraulic halt in a dimly lit hallway. B.D. started walking toward the massive wooden door at the end. Spencer stayed where he was. He reached into his pocket and gripped the jade bear.

"I assure you, Spencer Plain," B.D. growled. "The council is not feeling particularly patient at the moment. You need to come now."

Suddenly, a gravelly voice carried out of the council room. "We should send the boy *home*." It was Yude, the only Bearhaven bear Spencer *really* didn't like. When Spencer and Yude had met on Spencer's first night in Bearhaven, the bear gave Spencer a look he'd never forget: *You don't belong here.* It was no surprise Yude's voice was the loudest now. "He stranded a *cub* outside Bearhaven. He came here for his protection, but now it's time he *left* for ours."

Spencer felt a growl rising in his own throat. He stormed down the hall and into the council room. He wasn't about to let Yude have the last word, that was for sure.

12

The council room looked way more scary than the last time Spencer had been in it. For one thing, almost every bear sitting around the long wooden table that ran the whole length of the room was glaring at him.

Yude's lip was curled into a snarl. Mr. Bee, the school principal, seemed ready to give Spencer a furious lecture, and Raymond looked like he wanted to serve Spencer for dinner at Raymond's Cafe. Pinky, of Pinky's Rehab Center and Salon, wouldn't even look at Spencer. She knew better than anyone what harm could come to Kate outside Bearhaven's walls. Pinky's Rehab Center was the first stop for injured bears who were brought to Bearhaven, and it was Pinky's job to treat and care for them. Bearhaven's dentist, Dr. Dominica Fraser, flashed her teeth as she curled and uncurled her upper lip.

Grandmama Grizabelle was the only bear in the room who didn't look angry at the sight of Spencer. Instead, she looked disappointed, which was just as bad.

Each of the bears sat on one of the plush armchairs or couches arranged on either side of the long table. Spencer spotted the open couch where his parents were supposed to

sit during council meetings. He made his way over, realizing that Uncle Mark was watching Spencer, too, from one of the screens lining the wall at the end of the council table.

"I don't know what to say, Spence," Uncle Mark broke the silence. "What were you thinking?" He ran a hand through his hair.

"Isn't it obvious he *wasn't* thinking?" Yude cut in.

"That's not true!" Spencer shouted. His anger surged. "You've been lying to me about Mom and Dad. I heard you this morning. You haven't gotten *anywhere* in finding them." He glared at Uncle Mark. "And I know you want to just make me stay here and wait." He shot angry looks around the room. "I'm not a cub OR a prisoner, and you can't keep me locked up in Bearhaven! So I left. It's not my fault Kate followed me. I didn't know she was going to do that! She said

she was going to school." Spencer was furious and guilty at the same time. It was his fault Kate was missing right now, but the council needed to know it was *their* fault he'd had to leave Bearhaven in the first place.

"Spencer." Grandmama Grizabelle's voice was firm. "Under no circumstances do any of us approve of you sneaking out of Bearhaven. But I do understand why you did it." A few warning growls sounded around the room. "You were frustrated that no real progress has been made in finding your parents. And you were mad that we gave you false reports about their whereabouts. I know you were angry, however, your actions today have complicated things tremendously. You may have put a cub in grave danger, and that is absolutely unacceptable." Spencer looked down at the table. Grandmama Grizabelle was right.

"Start at the beginning, Mr. Plain," Mr. Bee instructed.

Without looking up, Spencer recounted the events of the day. He didn't leave anything out. Not even the part about pretending to be a Boy Scout, or the details Kirby told him about her controlled locations. He felt even more terrible with every word he said. It wasn't until he got to the end that he took his eyes off the table. He looked at Bunny, pleading. She had to see that this was all a big mistake! He *never* meant to put Kate in danger.

"When Kate jumped out, I didn't know what else to do. Her BEAR-COM was right there, pink and sparkling and everything. Kirby would've seen it in a second!"

The Bear Council erupted in a new wave of grumbles, and Yude muttered loudly, but Spencer pressed on. "I pretended I didn't know her . . . like she was a wild bear attacking us. I scared her away—"

"And where is she now?!" Bunny snarled. Her voice was filled with pain and the fur at the back of her neck was raised straight up in the air. Pinky reached a paw out to comfort the mother bear, but Bunny didn't seem to feel it. Spencer shrank back into his seat. He looked to the large screens at the front of the room for help.

"Bunny, please," Uncle Mark said. "I know this is difficult, but it's obvious Spencer only meant to keep Kate from being discovered. He should never have left Bearhaven, and he shouldn't have tampered with Bear Guard surveillance equipment, but none of his actions were intended to put Kate in danger."

"I was trying to protect her!" Spencer exclaimed, cutting off Yude's muttering.

"And it sounds like she was trying to protect *you*," Pinky added sadly.

Spencer rushed on. "I thought she'd come right home, then I'd explain and apologize. I was trying to make sure no one found Bearhaven—"

"B.D., the first search party has returned," Professor Weaver interrupted as he entered the room. Everyone froze. *Please say Kate's with them,* Spencer willed with all his might, but Professor Weaver had nothing more to say.

"I'll get their report." B.D. nodded to the professor as he left the room.

"Whatever your intentions may have been, Spencer," Professor Weaver said, "Kate is missing now. We've spoken to Reggie Russell, who informed us that he and Kate parted ways just before entering the school building. Kate told Reggie she'd smelled something wasn't right at home, and needed to return to check immediately. We can assume she smelled you leaving Bearhaven and followed you out. She has always had a very keen sense of smell, particularly where you are involved." Professor Weaver paused. "After carefully studying every single frame of footage taken by every single one of the Bear Guard's surveillance cameras, we've confirmed Kate never returned to Bearhaven. I am not blaming you, Spencer, and I don't think any of the other members of this council should blame you." He cast a look in Yude's direction. "But it is not acceptable—under any circumstances—that you snuck out of Bearhaven and interfered with the Bear Guard's security systems. You broke a lot of rules, and we will have to deal with that later. But right now, we need to focus on finding Kate, and we need to move quickly. It's only getting darker in those woods."

13

The council room buzzed with quiet discussion. Finding Kate was the most important thing, but the missing cub obviously wasn't the only problem. A BEAR-COM had never been unaccounted for outside Bearhaven's territory. Spencer understood all too well that if the high-tech translating device fell into the wrong hands, Bearhaven's secrets could be exposed and the community could be in huge trouble.

"Spencer," Uncle Mark broke through the chatter in the room. "I was hoping to talk to you about something on our call tonight, but now I don't think we'll have a chance to speak privately. I'm sorry we weren't honest with you about your parents' situation. That wasn't fair, you're right. Now that we're being honest . . ." Uncle Mark hesitated. *Uh-oh.* "There *has* been a lead about Jane and Shane." Spencer stared up at the screen at his uncle. He wanted to be happy to hear there was a lead, but could he trust that Uncle Mark was telling him the truth this time?

Suddenly, another screen on the wall of monitors where Uncle Mark's video feed was displayed blinked to life. It showed a single black-and-white photo.

"Jack, one of our contacts at a private airport sent me this picture. Your parents trained him to watch for anyone who might be illegally transporting bears. He alerts us if he suspects any foul play."

Spencer's heart immediately started to beat faster. If *this* was the lead, then things could be even worse than he'd imagined.

The image looked as though it had come from a security camera. There were three people in it and Spencer recognized all three immediately. First, he saw Margo and Ivan Lalicki, the evil sister and brother team who had captured Spencer during the mission to rescue Ro Ro and her cubs from Jay Grady's. Margo's greenish blond hair was sticking out from beneath her knitted cap.

Spencer shuddered, remembering how Margo and Ivan had put him in a cage, tied him up, and threatened him with bears whose actions they could control, to try to scare him into giving them information about Bearhaven. It hadn't worked. He hadn't told them anything.

In the front of the image Uncle Mark was projecting on the monitor, Spencer saw Pam, who was Margo and Ivan's boss and the creepiest person Spencer had ever seen in his life. Pam, the Bearhaven team had learned, was the mastermind of a huge network of evil and bear abuse. He was also holding Spencer's dad, Shane, prisoner.

Spencer shuddered again, recalling how he had seen his mother—working undercover, disguised as Pam's maid—for barely a minute, just before he was caught during a video call between Margo and Pam.

Standing next to Margo, Ivan strained, his muscled arms bulging, as he pulled something behind himself. Spencer ignored the shiny football helmet that always gleamed on Ivan's head and squinted, searching the object Ivan was pulling for any clues about what it was. It looked as if it could be a large shipping crate on wheels, but a velvety cloth was draped over the entire thing.

"What *is* that?"

"I don't know for certain, Spence, but Jack sent the picture because the crate is large enough to hold a live bear or a human. It's possible your Dad is in that crate and Pam is taking Shane to a new location. And if Shane is not in that crate, Pam and the Lalickis may be headed to wherever it is he's currently keeping your dad."

Spencer glared at the image on the screen. He grit his teeth imagining Dad inside the covered crate behind Ivan. "And Mom?"

"We haven't heard from her in a week," Uncle Mark answered solemnly. "I'm giving you all the information I have, Spence. The whole truth. Pam, Margo, and Ivan are on the move. They're transporting something, and they are keeping it concealed." Uncle Mark took a deep breath. "This picture was taken as they prepared to load a private plane that's registered to Pam. Jack couldn't give us any information about where they went after they'd passed the security camera that took the picture. He doesn't have access to the flight plans. My best bet is to figure out where their private plane landed after it left that airport. Hopefully, that will lead me straight to your parents."

Spencer opened his mouth to reply, but he couldn't think of anything to say. If Uncle Mark was going on a mission to find Mom and Dad, Spencer wanted to go with him. But there was Kate to think about . . . Now Spencer understood what Grandmama Grizabelle meant when she'd said he'd complicated things tremendously.

"I know this is a lot to process right now," Uncle Mark added.

A lot to process?! Between Kate's disappearance and Uncle Mark's new information about Mom and Dad, Spencer's head was spinning.

"I'm leaving on a solo mission to follow this lead as soon as our meeting here adjourns," Uncle Mark broke the silence. "I'll be cutting off contact with Bearhaven while I'm away."

"What do you mean 'cutting off contact'?" Spencer demanded. Most of the bears looked away.

"I'm going dark, Spence, for everyone's safety," Uncle Mark explained. "Your parents' and Bearhaven's, even mine and yours. Just try to remember this is a good thing. I really hope to come back with your parents."

"But I—" Spencer tried to protest, but just then, the sight of B.D. stalking back down the hallway silenced him and everyone else in the council room. Spencer knew the conversation was over. Now he had to return his attention to Kate.

B.D. didn't take his seat when he entered the room. He went to the head of the council table.

"The first search party did not find Kate," he addressed the room gravely. "In fact, they didn't find anything to suggest that Kate is still in the woods surrounding Bearhaven at all. What they did find were the scents of three humans." Bunny let out a low, rumbling growl. "We've identified one of the three: Kirby."

Spencer let out a deep sigh of relief. B.D. shot Spencer a stern look.

"Sorry," Spencer said. "But at least one of the three humans the Bear Guard smelled isn't a threat, right?" B.D.'s lip curled, and Spencer knew he was about to be scolded for interrupting the Head of the Guard's report. He sped on. "There's no way Kirby is responsible for Kate's disappearance, B.D. She might be a little too interested in gathering information about the woods surrounding Bearhaven, but I'm sure she'd never hurt a bear cub."

"Enough, Spencer," B.D. answered, then returned to updating the council. "The second and third humans couldn't be identified by the search party, but we're dealing with two adults. The guard determined that much."

"Excuse me, B.D.?" Spencer piped up. He didn't wait for B.D. to acknowledge him. He knew the bear wouldn't give him permission to speak, but the question burst from Spencer's mouth anyway. "Could it be Mom and Dad? Could they have escaped? They're two adult humans, right? Maybe *they* have Kate!" Spencer searched B.D.'s face, willing the bear to say it was possible.

"I'm afraid not, Spencer," B.D. answered right away. "Our Bear Guard has had enough contact with your parents to identify their scents immediately."

Spencer swallowed hard, trying to ignore the huge lump in his throat. *Uncle Mark is leaving to find Mom and Dad as soon as this meeting is over,* he reminded himself.

B.D. pressed on. "We have three situations to deal with now. First, there has been a lead in the search for Jane and Shane Plain: the photo Mark showed us. Second, a cub, Kate Weaver, has disappeared from the woods outside Bearhaven, and third, two unidentified humans in addition to Kirby have been smelled at the perimeter. Mark will be departing shortly on a solo mission to continue the search for Jane and Shane. As for Kate's disappearance, I've already dispatched a guard member to find Kirby and watch for any signs of her involvement. We will work to find more clues about who the two adult humans are, what their intentions for being here were, and what they've done with Kate." Bunny growled again.

Spencer looked down at the council table. He didn't want to think about what two unknown humans would have done with Kate. The most likely option was the most terrifying. He shook the thought away. There weren't hunters in the woods outside Bearhaven. There couldn't be.

"As for the threat of a security breach that the unidentified humans pose . . ." B.D. rose onto his hind legs. He towered over the council. "Bearhaven is on lockdown. Effective immediately."

14

Spencer stepped out of the Lab and into the pitch-black night. Bearhaven was dark. Much darker than he'd ever seen it. The lights that usually illuminated the Lab were off; so was the lantern that lit the head of the path back to Bearhaven's center.

"Aldo," Spencer whispered into the dark, afraid to break the silence that seemed to have fallen over the entire valley.

"I'm right behind you, little man," Aldo answered, then stepped up to Spencer's side. Spencer could just make out the bear. "Welcome to lockdown mode."

"All the lights go off?" Spencer asked.

"The outdoor lights do. This is a Level Two Lockdown. Bears can keep the lights on in their houses, and there is a curfew; everyone is supposed to stay inside after dark. Come on, we should get home." The bear hurried toward the path that would take them back to the Weavers' house. In the dark, Spencer could barely see where they were going. He broke into a jog to keep up with the shadow he knew was Aldo.

Bearhaven seemed deserted. It wasn't until they passed the glowing windows at Raymond's that Spencer saw any proof the bears were still here at all. The dining room was illuminated, but the tables were mostly empty. A few bears were sitting in front of platters of half-eaten food, deep in what looked like worried conversation.

"Aldo, how did everyone know to go into lockdown mode?" Spencer asked.

"A message came through our BEAR-COMs. You were still in the council meeting. I guess since B.D. made the decision, the council heard it directly from him."

"Oh, yeah." Spencer wondered what the council was discussing now. Their meeting was still going on in the Lab, but Aldo had been right. Everyone felt like Spencer had already done enough. They did not want his help. Instead, they had dismissed him, sending him back to the Weavers'.

Aldo hurried up the Weavers' front path and pushed open the front door. He stepped inside and swung his head from side to side, sniffing rapidly. Spencer could tell the bear hoped his younger sister had returned while they were gone.

She hadn't.

Spencer stepped into the honey-colored living room and closed the door behind them. Lisle was standing beside the fireplace. She glanced at Spencer but looked away without saying anything.

"What's going on?" she asked her brother. "The lockdown message said there were humans at the perimeter."

"Three humans were smelled in the woods right outside Bearhaven."

"And Kate?" Lisle asked.

"No sign of her."

"That's all the information?" Lisle asked. "Kate's still out there all alone?"

"So far," Aldo answered. "I looked at footage from all the surveillance cameras myself. There's nothing there."

"Lisle, I—" Spencer wanted to apologize for the part he'd played in Kate's disappearance, but Lisle cut him off.

"Let's just focus on Kate's safe return, Spencer." Lisle's voice was quiet. She seemed exhausted and barely looked at him when she spoke. She tried to cover a yawn.

"You should get some rest," Aldo said. He moved to stoke the fire. "I'll stay up in case Kate comes home."

"Wake me if you hear anything?"

Aldo nodded. Lisle padded toward the stairs, heading to the room she shared with Kate.

After a moment, Spencer spoke up.

"I think Kirby can help us," he said, sitting on the couch facing the massive stone fireplace. "I know she's technically a suspect, but she didn't do anything to Kate. She was *with me* when Kate ran into the woods. She could have information the Bear Guard doesn't. She has her own cameras and surveillance all over the woods. She spends *all* her time watching the forest, Aldo. She *must* have seen something."

"Did you tell this to B.D.?"

"I tried." Spencer shrugged. "He doesn't want to listen to me right now. Nobody does . . ."

Aldo paced. "Okay. I'm listening."

Spencer took a deep breath and sat up straight. "Let's go to Kirby. You and me." Aldo stopped pacing and stared into the fire. Spencer rushed on. "There's no way I'll be able to sneak out of Bearhaven again by myself, especially with the lockdown. Besides, it takes way too long and they're going to be watching me *and* the security cameras more carefully than ever. The only way is if you take me up over the bridge in the trees."

"I could lose my cuffs," Aldo said without turning around.

"You could save your sister," Spencer said.

Aldo looked down at the silver cuffs on his front legs. Spencer knew how proud the bear was of his position in the Bear Guard. It took a lot of training and hard work to earn the right to wear those cuffs. Kate said Aldo made sure to shine his cuffs every night before bed, and from the way they gleamed, Spencer was sure it was true.

They lapsed into silence. The sound of the fire crackled through the room. Spencer's stomach growled. He hadn't eaten since breakfast. He tried to ignore his hunger, waiting for Aldo's answer.

After a long moment, Spencer's stomach growled again. He moved toward the kitchen, ready to climb up onto the bears' stone counter and find some food. Then Aldo started talking.

"When I got onto the Bear Guard, Kate was more excited than anyone. She baked a dandelion cake just for me, you know. It was really sweet, but also a little terrible because then I had to eat it . . ." Spencer held his breath. He was afraid to interrupt Aldo. The bear seemed to be thinking aloud. "Kate's not a very good cook, even though she wants to be, but she was so excited to hear that I was getting my cuffs that she ran home from school and made a mess of the kitchen before anyone else got here."

Spencer laughed, then stopped himself. He didn't think the bear was trying to be funny.

Aldo turned around to face Spencer. "I ate every bite of that gross cake. It wasn't even that bad, because I knew how happy it made Kate."

Spencer swallowed hard. *Does this mean he'll take me to Kirby?* He didn't ask, afraid to push the bear. He didn't have to; Aldo started talking again.

"I'll do whatever I can to get my little sister back."

"So you're saying—"

Aldo cut him off. "How do we find Kirby?"

Spencer pulled the crumpled-up piece of notebook paper from his pocket. "Did they teach you how to read coordinates in guard training?"

15

The alarm on Spencer's cell phone went off at six fifteen the next morning, but he was already awake. In fact, he hadn't slept a wink all night. He turned off the silent, vibrating alarm and checked to make sure the phone was charging. He took one last look at the open atlas on his bedroom floor and the map lying beside it. *Cheng and his Boy Scout friends would be impressed,* Spencer thought. He'd spent the night using the atlas to draw a path to Kirby's house on a paper map of the area Aldo had given him. He had used Kirby's coordinates to locate her house in the atlas, then he'd compared its location with Aldo's map, which didn't have the latitude and longitude marked. He'd drawn a big red *X* over the spot where Kirby's house should be.

Spencer closed the atlas and returned it to his bookshelf. He was just folding the paper map and stuffing it into his backpack when there was a light tap on the door. He opened the door a crack. Aldo was in the hallway looking nervously from side to side.

"There hasn't been any update," Aldo reported quietly. He stepped into Spencer's bedroom. Aldo and Spencer had agreed to go to Kirby if the Bear Council and Bear Guard hadn't made any progress in finding Kate overnight. Now, Spencer's excitement began to build. They were going on their own mission. They were going to help find Kate!

"Mom hasn't come home yet, and Dad was in the Lab with her most of the night, but he just got back and fell asleep upstairs on the couch. We'll have to get past him on our way out." The bear turned to lead the way, but Spencer stopped him.

"Aldo, your cuffs . . ." Last night, Spencer had prepared for this trip to Kirby's by reviewing the things he'd seen B.D. and Uncle Mark do right before the rescue mission to Jay Grady's—the only mission Spencer had ever been on. And B.D. had taken his cuffs off before leaving the TUBE. He'd said it would be too dangerous to wear the cuffs in public.

At the very least, without his cuffs it would be easier for Aldo to move through the woods unnoticed, and less suspicious if he happened to be seen. "You can leave them in here." Spencer opened one of his dresser drawers and motioned to the soft piles of folded clothing inside. "They'll be safe until we get back."

Aldo hesitated. *He probably hasn't taken them off since he became a member of the Bear Guard,* Spencer realized. After a moment, the bear extended a paw over the clothing in Spencer's dresser. He used the claws of one front paw to push the cuff off the other. Spencer thought he saw Aldo flinch when the gleaming silver cuff hit the clothing in the drawer. "This better work," Aldo said, forcing a smile and moving on to the second cuff.

I know, Spencer wanted to answer. *Trust me, I know.* "It

will," he said as he nestled the silver cuffs down between two piles of sweatshirts.

Spencer closed the drawer before Aldo could change his mind about leaving the cuffs behind. He slung his backpack onto his back. They set off down the hallway. All the bedroom doors were shut tight. The giant screen in the family room that was usually filled with *Salmon King*'s flashing fins and leaping bears was dark. Spencer had never heard the Weavers' house so quiet.

When Aldo started to climb the stairs, Spencer realized the difference between his own silent walking that he practiced in STORM training and the silent walking of a trained member of the Bear Guard. Aldo moved his large body up the stairs without any sound at all. But when Spencer stepped onto the bottom stair, his sneaker hit the stone with a faint thud. Aldo's ears snapped to attention. Spencer didn't move. The bear returned to the bottom of the stairs just as silently as he'd gone up. When he reached Spencer, he lowered his belly to the floor and motioned for Spencer to climb onto his back.

Spencer wanted to protest. He didn't need help! He could do silent walking. He'd trained for this! But he was afraid to wake up Professor Weaver. He grabbed the soft fur at Aldo's neck with both hands and climbed onto the bear's back. As soon as Spencer had a tight grip on Aldo, they crept up the stairs in just a few seconds. They passed through the living room without waking the professor, opened the heavy front door, and stepped out onto the Weavers' front path. Without warning, Aldo broke into a gallop.

"Aldo!" Spencer hissed, bumping against the bear's back as they tore through Bearhaven. He held on with all his might, squeezing Aldo's body with his legs. "Aldo!" he whispered again. This wasn't what Spencer had in mind for their mission. He'd thought they'd be more like two undercover operatives, silent walking, sneaking through Bearhaven side by side.

Spencer could only see their progress in brief glances as they left the town behind and broke out into the valley. Every time he tried to lift his head to look around, the bear's black-and-tan fur filled his eyes. He felt Aldo start up a steep hill. *We're almost to the clearing!* Even though Spencer had expected to sneak out of Bearhaven on his own two legs, he had to admit they were moving much faster this way, and riding a bear wasn't the worst way to travel.

"Hold on tight, now!" Aldo called. Spencer lifted his head to check their surroundings. The clearing was just a few paces ahead. Aldo wasn't slowing down. *Wait . . .* Spencer thought as his view got blocked by fur. *We can't take the tree elevator up to the bridge above the trees. That will give us away in a minute!* The Bear Guard would be alerted as soon as the elevator was in use, but it looked like Aldo had already figured that out.

"Aldo, wait!" Spencer cried. He tightened his grip on the bear just in time. Aldo launched himself at one of the trees and began to climb at a pace that only a young, trained member of the Bear Guard would be able to manage. Leaves and air whipped past Spencer as they climbed high into the tree. He tried to scream but his mouth filled with fur. They were going too fast! It was getting harder to hold on. The familiar images Spencer couldn't explain suddenly filled his head: leaves and branches snapping back into place as he fell through them. Now, this time, he also saw a bear's face—*Yude*.

Before Spencer could react, the climb was over. Aldo hopped onto the bridge and came to a stop, breathing heavily.

"You all right up there?" the bear asked almost casually once he'd caught his breath.

"You didn't tell me we were going to do that!" Spencer yelled, trying to recover. How had the plan he'd made so carefully to sneak out of Bearhaven gone so haywire?

"What did you think we were going to do?" Aldo sounded surprised. "You said you needed me to bring you over the bridge."

"I didn't—I thought—you should have warned me!" Spencer sputtered. It didn't matter. They were above the trees now. "There isn't a camera up here?" He scanned the nearby branches for a fake beehive.

"Not right here. There's one on the other side, but we're in a blind spot. Sorry if I scared you," Aldo added. "I thought I was just following the plan." He started to pad across the bridge. "I'm going to jump onto a tree trunk to our left in a few steps. That way the camera won't see us. I'll climb to the ground from there, all right?"

Spencer took a deep breath. He didn't see any other option. "All right." A moment later they were in the air. There was a thud as Aldo made perfect contact with a tree. They started to descend.

16

Spencer slipped down off Aldo's back. "That's better," he muttered, glad to have his feet on the ground again. The trip down from the bridge in the trees hadn't been as bad as the trip up, but Spencer was happy it was over. He took off his backpack and pulled out the map he'd drawn. The sooner they set off toward Kirby's, the better.

Aldo stretched and shook out his fur. "The sun's coming up," he said. He rose onto his hind legs to inspect the woods. "Smells like the coast is clear. How far is Kirby's?"

"A couple of miles, if my map's right." Spencer laid the map on the ground between them and took out his phone. "We need to start going south." He tapped his compass app and waited for it to load.

"That's this way." Aldo dropped back to all fours and walked a few paces in one direction. The compass app finally loaded, confirming the direction Aldo was heading was definitely south.

"Impressive!" Spencer picked up his map and followed Aldo into the woods. *This might be easier than I thought.* Spencer consulted his map as they walked. By the time they reached the edge of a large open field, the sun had finished rising, and Spencer and Aldo's stomachs were both growling for breakfast.

"If my research on coordinates was right, we should be really close now." Spencer consulted the map.

Aldo rose up onto his hind legs and sniffed hard. "You're right," he said after a moment. "Kirby's around here somewhere. At least, a human that's not *you* is around here somewhere."

Spencer pored over his map. The red *X* he'd marked was on one side of this clearing. "Now we need to head east!" he exclaimed. "Come on!" Spencer slung his backpack over one shoulder and started to jog into the woods with the map crumpled in his arms.

"This way, little man," Aldo called, nodding his head in the opposite direction.

"Oh. Right," Spencer said sheepishly. He followed Aldo, now heading east. *Do bears have internal compasses?* he wondered, trying to remember if his parents had ever told him that. Mom and Dad loved to tell him stories and facts about bears, and Spencer knew way more about the animals than any of the other kids back home, but he couldn't remember ever hearing anything about bears' incredible sense of direction.

He was about to ask Aldo when he was suddenly met with a face full of fur. Aldo had stopped walking. Spencer poked his head around the side of the bear.

Just ahead, a small white house sat surrounded by trees. Its paint was weathered and peeling, and the porch in the front was supported by cinder blocks. A narrow dirt driveway curled off into the woods, but there wasn't a single car parked in it. The house looked abandoned. The huge satellite dish perched on top of the rusting metal roof was the only sign anyone might really be living there.

"I guess this is it," Spencer whispered. He tried to step around Aldo, but the bear blocked his path.

"Not so fast," Aldo said, nudging Spencer backward. "You can't go marching in there holding a map straight to Bearhaven."

"Oh, right . . ." Spencer stuffed the map inside his backpack. His excitement kicked in again.

"And remember, you're here to *get* information, not give it. Got it?"

"Got it. You'll be here?"

Aldo inspected the cluster of trees they were standing in, then shook his head. "I'll be up there." He gestured with his snout toward the thick canopy of leaves above them. "Good luck," he added, before taking Spencer's backpack in his teeth and climbing a nearby tree. After a minute, Spencer couldn't spot the bear at all in the tree's branches.

Spencer jogged toward the house. He mounted the porch stairs slowly, then stepped up to the front door.

Beep beep beep beep.

Spencer froze. He searched the front door for something that might have made the electronic sound.

Beep beep beep beep.

There it was again! This time, Spencer saw that the noise was coming from a small camera perched on a metal shelf above one of the windows. A long black cord ran from the camera into the house. *Kirby definitely lives here.*

"Uh . . . Kirby?" Spencer called. He knocked once on

the door. Before his fist could hit the door a second time, it flew open.

"Hey!" Kirby shouted, ducking to avoid Spencer's fist.

"Oh! Sorry! I survived," he blurted out. Kirby stared at him. "I'm going to get my Scout badge."

"I know you're not a Boy Scout," Kirby answered matter-of-factly. "I've known all along. Why don't you tell me who you *really* are?"

"If you knew I wasn't a Boy Scout, then why did you tell me where to find your house?" Spencer shot back.

"Because you owe me information, remember?" Kirby scanned the trees behind Spencer. He shifted, trying to block her view. "Some very strange things have developed over the last twenty-four hours, and I'm—"

"That's why I'm here!" Spencer interrupted. If Kirby had information, Spencer needed it *now*.

Kirby's eyes snapped back to Spencer. "You know something?"

"Well actually, I was hoping *you* might know something . . . I need your help."

"You need information? From me? About the woods?" Kirby's voice was hopeful.

"Yes."

"You've come to the right place." Kirby swung opened the door, revealing the front room of her house, and Spencer stepped inside.

17

Kate would love this place, Spencer thought. He took a long look around Kirby's living room. Everything was sparkly or candy-colored, and bunches of fake pink flowers were scattered around. When Spencer looked closer, he saw that most of the flower arrangements were covered with dust. The whole room looked neglected—like no one had time or interest to keep it tidy. The couch was the only place to sit and it was piled high with fluffy pillows.

"My mom gets all this pink, sparkly stuff for free from work," Kirby explained. "She sells craft supplies. She likes flowers and frilly things anyway. I don't like it very much, but I stay in my room a lot, and *that* looks just the way I want it to. Come on, I'll show you." Kirby turned on her heels and led Spencer to a door at the end of a narrow hallway.

He followed her into a small bedroom filled with electronics, video equipment, and very old-looking computers. A large wooden desk took up most of the room, and what seemed to be the only working computer sat in the middle of it. The computer was connected to a DVD player and various other homemade-looking contraptions Spencer couldn't identify.

Kirby dropped into the chair at the desk and wiggled her mouse, illuminating her computer screen.

The image that appeared was of Spencer. He jumped back, surprised.

"It's from the security camera on the porch," Kirby explained. "It takes a picture of anyone who walks up the front steps."

That explains the beeping camera, Spencer thought.

"So, anyway," Kirby said, moving on. "What do you want to know?"

Spencer wished he and Aldo had prepared questions to ask Kirby. Now that he was here, he was afraid he'd say the wrong thing and cause more problems for Bearhaven. "That bear we saw yesterday, did you happen to see any other signs of her anywhere?"

"Her?" Kirby spun her chair around to stare at Spencer. *Oh, great.* "It."

"You said 'her.' How do you know the bear is a her?"

"I don't. I was just wondering if you knew anything else about that bear. It's really important."

"What else do *you* know about that bear?"

"I, uh . . ." Spencer stumbled. *Pull it together!* Kirby raised her eyebrows. "I know her," he finally said. Kirby straightened up.

"What do you mean you *know* her?"

"I'm friends with her, and she's missing, and I really need to know if you have any clues that might help me find her." Spencer stopped himself from saying anything else.

"You're *friends* with a *bear*? Is there something . . . different about this bear? I *knew* there was something weird going on in these woods! And I *knew* it had something to do with bears! There have been so many signs to—"

"No!" Spencer practically shouted. He was not about to give Kirby any more clues about Bearhaven. He'd already said enough. "She's just a regular wild bear, but we're friends."

"Then why did you scare her away yesterday?" Kirby narrowed her eyes, inspecting him even more carefully now.

"I was afraid you might . . . hurt her."

"I would never hurt a bear! I promise! Can *I* be friends with her, too? Please?"

"Well, I don't know where she is right now . . ." This wasn't going as well as Spencer had hoped. When was Kirby going to give up the questioning and help him?

"If I help you, then can I be friends with her?" Kirby pressed.

"KIRBY!" Spencer yelled. "This is kind of an emergency!"

Kirby spun her chair back around to face her computer.

"All right, all right. You didn't say it was an emergency before." She started to open files and sift through images. Spencer took a deep breath. *Now we're getting somewhere.*

"What did you mean when you said things had developed over the last twenty-four hours?" Spencer stood behind Kirby to get a better view of the screen.

"I check my surveillance cameras, microphone, and controlled locations every day. Usually, I only find anything unusual or something that requires further investigation once a week. I only have clues at more than one of my surveillance locations at the same time maybe once every *month*. Yesterday, after I left you, I had evidence to collect from one camera, the microphone, *and* one controlled location! That much activity *must* mean something! Look at this . . ."

Kirby opened a file on her computer. The first frame of a video appeared on the screen. When she pressed PLAY Spencer saw a sudden flash of silver between two trees. It definitely wasn't Kate, but what was it?

"What *is* that?!" He leaned closer to the screen. "Play it again."

"Here. I'll slow it down so you can get a better look," Kirby said, then restarted the video clip. This time, the video played in slow motion. Spencer could make out a silver van as it flashed into the frame and then out again.

"Whoa!" Spencer could hardly believe it. Kirby really *did* have information they needed! "Can you slow it down any more than that?"

Kirby didn't answer. She just fiddled around with the settings on her computer, then hit PLAY again.

"Can you freeze it? When the license plate comes into view?"

"Of course," Kirby answered, though it took her a few tries before they could get a clean freeze-frame of the license plate.

"The van's from Florida," Kirby said, pointing at the screen. "See the oranges?" She was right. In the middle of the license plate number there was a pair of oranges.

"Do you have a printer?" Spencer asked. He *had* to show this to B.D. It was definitely a lead.

Kirby popped up from her chair and pulled something that looked like it could have once been a printer down from a shelf. She grabbed a second contraption and put it down on the desk. She got a little bundle of cables out of a drawer and started to connect the two pieces of equipment together before connecting them both to the computer.

"Where do you get all this stuff?" Spencer asked. It looked as if Kirby was creating computers out of printers, radios out of cameras, and microphones out of stereos, and vice versa. He was impressed, and a little jealous of all Kirby's cool equipment.

"My dad sends it to me from California. He's a bodyguard in Hollywood. They use a lot of equipment," Kirby answered, rearranging some of the cables after her first attempt to print didn't produce anything. "The stuff he sends me is old and it usually doesn't work at first, or it comes in pieces, but I learn how to fix everything on the Internet. There!" One of the printers erupted in sound as it started to work. Kirby settled back into her seat at the desk. "Want to hear the audio my hidden microphone picked up? It sounds very strange."

When Spencer heard what Kirby's hidden microphone had recorded, the hair on his arms stood up.

Kirby's recording filled the room with a piercing, high-pitched cry. It was the sound of a black bear cub in distress. It was Kate crying for help.

Kirby played it again, and Spencer cringed.

Kate's in trouble. There was no doubt about it. Cubs only made that sound when they thought they were facing terrible danger.

"Isn't it weird? I can't make any sense of it."

"Yeah, I've never heard anything like it . . ." Spencer muttered. He reached for the printout of the license plate. "Can I take this?"

Kirby hesitated.

"So what did you see at the controlled location?" he asked, moving on before Kirby could refuse him the printout. It worked. Kirby pulled a metal lockbox out from behind her computer. She shoved a pile of cables and tools aside to clear a space at the front of the desk and carefully set the box down. A combination lock dangled from the front of the box.

"Can you please turn around?" Kirby asked, her fingers poised over the lock.

"Oh, sure." Spencer turned around, listening to the spinning sound of Kirby entering the lock's combination.

Click!

Spencer turned back to the desk, dying to see what else Kirby had found that might lead to Kate.

At first he was confused. A plaid scarf was neatly folded inside the box. But it was almost May; nobody would have needed a scarf yesterday.

Kirby laughed. "That's just an old scarf. It's keeping the contraption safe." Kirby gingerly unfolded the scarf, revealing what it covered.

Spencer gasped, then faked a cough to hide his shock. He stepped closer. Kate's BEAR-COM glittered pink from within the folds of Kirby's scarf. A paper tag had been tied to the BEAR-COM with a string. *Exhibit A.*

18

"Can I use your bathroom?" Spencer blurted out. Kirby was studying his face, waiting for him to react to her most exciting finding: Exhibit A, Kate's BEAR-COM. He couldn't think with her staring at him like that, and he *definitely* couldn't trust himself not to give away the fact he knew exactly what the BEAR-COM was and where it came from. He needed a minute to collect himself.

"Yeah, sure." Kirby sounded disappointed. She directed Spencer to the bathroom just down the hall.

Spencer stepped into the tiny blue-tiled bathroom and closed the door. He looked around, trying to calm down. Beyond the peeling blue-and-white striped wallpaper, there wasn't much to look at. Spencer stared into the mirror.

"I have to steal Kate's BEAR-COM from that box," he whispered to his reflection, his mind racing. "But how?" Kirby was determined to solve the mystery of the bears in the woods, and the BEAR-COM was obviously her most prized finding yet, even if she didn't know what it was. Sneaking the BEAR-COM out of here without her noticing would never work, Kirby was way too smart for that, but leaving the device with her wasn't an option. Spencer had no choice but to come up with something. He had to bring that BEAR-COM back to Bearhaven, and he needed to get the image of the van back to the council right away.

Spencer couldn't believe how lucky he and everyone in Bearhaven were that Kate's captors didn't have her BEAR-COM. Bearhaven's most important technology would remain a secret, as long as Spencer could get it out of Kirby's lockbox . . .

Spencer focused on his reflection in the mirror. He needed to think like an operative. He needed a plan.

In Operative Communications, Aldo had told Spencer about a device called the Ear-COM that Bearhaven operatives used on special missions, sort of a mini version of the BEAR-COM. It was a hidden earpiece both bears and humans could wear so they could still communicate without the risk of exposing the BEAR-COM technology. Spencer wished he and Aldo had Ear-COMs for this mission; then Aldo could just tell him what to do next.

"Spencer?" Kirby called.

"I'll be right out!" Spencer flushed the toilet so Kirby wouldn't get suspicious.

Aldo had also explained that effective Operative Communications wasn't just about using Bearhaven's high-tech translation gear. It was also about knowing your operative team's strengths and weaknesses. And about what you were willing to risk to get the results you needed. Spencer reviewed the details of the mission. As a team, he and Aldo had an advantage over Kirby, mostly because of Aldo's physical strength and speed. Their team's weakness was they didn't want Kirby to see Aldo and they needed to keep Bearhaven a total secret. Spencer's mind raced. But even if Kirby saw Spencer and Aldo together, she wouldn't be able to catch them and follow them to Bearhaven. This was an emergency. They were going to have to risk something, and the most important thing was getting back to Bearhaven with Kate's BEAR-COM and Kirby's other leads.

A plan started to take shape in Spencer's mind. He washed his hands and left the bathroom.

"All right, so I've gone over all the evidence again," Kirby said as Spencer joined her. While she was talking, he quickly reviewed the layout of her room. He was standing in the doorway facing Kirby, who sat at her desk, the lockbox beside her. As soon as Kirby turned to her computer, her back would be to him. The room was small, but Spencer thought that was a good thing. If he situated himself between Kirby and her desk, he would be in her way. She wouldn't be able to get back to the lockbox until he moved back to the door. "There's the van I caught on camera and the mysterious sound my mic picked up. Then there's the sparkly contraption I found at the controlled location. I think what we should do first is check my notes on the controlled locations for the past few days, just in case—"

"Actually, can I watch the video of the van again?" Spencer cut her off. Adrenaline was already starting to pump into his veins.

"Yup, no problemo." Kirby focused on her computer, turning her back to Spencer. Just as she pressed PLAY to show the surveillance video, Spencer hit the power buttons on the three closest machines. They blared to life. One, a radio, blasted crackly pop music; the second made the high-pitched beeping sounds of a fax machine, and the third clicked and whirred really loudly.

Kirby spun around and launched herself out of her chair. "What are you doing?!" she shouted, trying to get to the machines Spencer had turned on. The room was too small. Spencer was in her way.

"Sorry! I just wanted to see what all your cool equipment does!" The blaring noise continued, filling the room. Kirby pushed past Spencer and he stepped out of her way. He moved toward her computer, and the open lockbox next to it, making space for Kirby to get to her contraptions. As quickly as he could, while Kirby shut down her equipment, Spencer grabbed the BEAR-COM and shoved it into his back pocket.

The pop music cut out first, then the other two machines fell silent. Kirby turned back to Spencer. "You aren't allowed to touch *anything*!" she scolded. "This equipment is very carefully put together and it's *not* as easy as you think to get everything working right. Not to mention the fact that you don't know what they do!" She crossed her arms and glared at Spencer.

"I'm sorry, Kirby. I, uh . . . I just got excited . . . about all of the information you collected. Really, sorry. Here . . ." He motioned for Kirby to return to her seat at the computer. "Can we go over your notes now?"

Kirby pursed her lips as she squeezed past Spencer. He took a few steps backward, closing the distance between himself and the door as much as possible. His heart raced as he watched her take her seat. It was now or never. The second Kirby was seated at her desk, leaning toward the lockbox, he turned and ran.

"Hey!"

Spencer didn't stop. He heard Kirby's desk chair bang against something.

"STOP!" she yelled, but he was already throwing open her front door. He crossed the creaking porch in a single stride and skipped the steps altogether, jumping to the ground. He heard the door slam shut, then swing open again. Kirby was close behind him.

"ALDO!!!" he yelled. Up ahead, he saw a great black mass jump to the ground from the lowest branches of a tree.

"AHHH!" Kirby screamed behind him. Spencer ran faster. Aldo crouched down, facing away from Spencer and Kirby. His BEAR-COM was hidden from sight by the rest of his body. He'd dropped Spencer's backpack to the ground nearby. Running as fast as he could, Spencer scooped up the backpack. He didn't break his stride as he swung the bag onto his back.

Spencer took two more steps, then leaped up onto Aldo. He scrambled to get into the right position, wrapping his legs tightly around the bear and grabbing fistfuls of fur.

"Now," he said under his breath. Aldo lurched forward, then broke into a sprint.

"Wait!" Spencer heard Kirby cry from behind him. The sound of her footsteps picked up again, but it was no use. Aldo was tearing through the woods at a terrifying speed. There was no way Kirby would ever catch up.

19

Spencer buried his face in Aldo's fur and held on tightly as they raced through the woods toward the wall of trees surrounding Bearhaven. He could still feel the adrenaline coursing through his veins from the escape from Kirby's as he reviewed all her evidence. Spencer was so deep in thought he barely noticed when they flew up the trunk of a tall tree, over the small bridge, and down into the clearing just inside Bearhaven's walls.

Aldo skidded to a stop in the clearing.

Spencer slid off the bear's back. He wanted to get this information to the council as quickly as possible, but he knew he owed Aldo an explanation for what just happened.

"For the record, that was *not* what I meant when I told you not to give anything away to Kirby!" Aldo panted. "Usually humans don't ride bears around the woods! Tell me you got something that will make exposing me and you riding off on my back worth it."

"I did! Kirby had Kate's BEAR-COM! I couldn't think of any other way to get it back here. We had to make a break for it. And . . . well . . ." Spencer hesitated. He didn't want Aldo to be mad at him, but he figured he'd better tell the bear everything. "I accidentally told her that I was friends with Kate," he blurted out. "I didn't say anything about Bearhaven or the BEAR-COMs or anything like that but I admitted that I was friends with a bear in the wild. So I thought maybe escaping with a bear wouldn't really be revealing too much more than she already knew." Spencer stopped himself from saying more, but really, letting Kirby see Aldo made Spencer feel a little less guilty about stealing the BEAR-COM back from her.

Aldo paced back and forth, deep in thought. "You said you have Kate's BEAR-COM?"

Spencer nodded, pulling the sparkly pink device out of his back pocket.

"Anything else? Any leads?"

"Yes, I got—"

"Hop on." Aldo crouched down. "You can show me when you show the council. Let's keep the part about telling Kirby you're friends with bears to ourselves though, okay? And the part about our getaway."

"You got it," Spencer answered. "Thanks, Aldo." He shoved the BEAR-COM back into his pocket and climbed onto Aldo's back. As soon as he'd gotten a good hold of Aldo's fur, the bear took off toward the Lab. By the time they started down the path to the riverside, they were moving so quickly that other bears had to jump out of the way to avoid being trampled.

They broke into the clearing that housed Bearhaven's top-secret lab. Aldo sprinted straight at the metal wall of the great dome structure. He blew air out in a huge puff to create a hole in the special metal, then leaped through the opening.

He hit the transparent film with so much force that they burst right through. Spencer stayed plastered to Aldo's back. He made himself as small as possible, afraid he'd be skimmed off by the closing wall.

They slid to a stop inside the Lab's lobby. Breathing heavily, Aldo lowered his body to the ground to let Spencer get down. Spencer scrambled to the floor.

"Hey!" A member of the Bear Guard who Spencer didn't recognize stepped out of the surveillance room and started toward them. *Uh-oh* . . . "He's not authorized to be in here." The bear swung his head in Spencer's direction.

Aldo opened his mouth to respond, but, just then, Professor Weaver stepped out into the hall. Aldo's mouth snapped shut at the sight of his father.

"I'll handle this, thank you." Professor Weaver called off the guard. "I'm glad you're both safe." He fixed Spencer and Aldo with a stern look. He didn't seem very glad. "And I certainly hope you two have a good explanation for this. Bunny has been an absolute wreck thinking we'd lost the both of you as well. We were just about to send a search party after *you*."

"We do have a good explanation," Aldo answered quickly, rushing down the hall. "And we need to speak to B.D. and the whole council if they're here."

"They're here," Professor Weaver answered, dropping his reprimanding tone. "Three search parties have come back empty-handed. All we have is the scent of Kirby and two other unidentified humans."

"We have more!" Spencer exclaimed. He turned into the Bear Guard's surveillance room and followed Professor Weaver and Aldo onto the platform that would bring them down to the private floor below. Professor Weaver hit the button.

Whoosh!

Before the platform had come to a stop, Spencer hopped off and ran toward the council room. Bunny's voice thundered out into the hall.

"What do you *mean* the Bear Guard hasn't found anything?! What is the guard trained for if not situations like this, B.D.?"

"We found something!" Spencer shouted. He burst into the council meeting with Aldo and Professor Weaver right behind him. "Aldo and I found something!"

The council members erupted in protests but Spencer ignored them. He tore off his backpack and retrieved the picture of the van's license plate. He slapped it down on the table. "I saw video footage of a van with this license plate driving through the woods outside Bearhaven."

"Where did you get this?" Bunny asked, rushing over to examine the picture.

"One of Kirby's cameras," Spencer answered.

"*Kirby?* You're sure she can be trusted?" B.D. loped around to get a better look at the picture.

Spencer nodded vigorously. "One hundred percent." He looked up at the wall of computer monitors in the front of the room. Evarita was on one of the screens, but the rest of the monitors were dark. She gave Spencer a thumbs-up.

"Where's Uncle Mark?" Spencer asked, realizing as the words came out of his mouth he already knew the answer. The room fell silent.

"He left on the mission last night and cut off communication this morning," Evarita answered. "He told us last night, Spencer. Don't you remember?"

"I remember. But . . ." Spencer felt a lump rising in his throat. "I thought I'd get to say good-bye or something."

"I'd say you forfeited your good-byes when you snuck out of Bearhaven for the *second* time in twenty-four hours," Yude snarled.

"Oh, shush, Yude," Dominica Fraser broke in. "Thanks to Spencer and Aldo sneaking out we're finally getting somewhere."

"Hopefully, he won't be gone long," Evarita said, ignoring Yude's comment. "And when he returns he could have your parents with him."

Spencer swallowed hard. *Focus on Kate,* he told himself. Uncle Mark would take care of bringing Mom and Dad home. He had to.

"There's more," Aldo said, returning everyone's attention to the issue at hand: Kate.

"We got Kate's BEAR-COM back." Spencer reached into his back pocket, and then carefully laid the device on the table. "The strap is broken. I think it must have fallen off when she ran away from me. The Exhibit A tag is Kirby's." Bunny's head darted toward the device, her snout sniffing every inch of the pink rhinestone-covered BEAR-COM. She squeezed her eyes shut and took a deep breath. Spencer looked away. He couldn't stand to see Bunny look so sad. He wouldn't tell the whole council what Kirby's microphone had recorded. It was bad enough he had heard the sounds of Kate in distress on Kirby's recording. Telling Bunny about Kate's cry now wouldn't do anyone any good.

"Evarita, are you ready to look up that license plate?" B.D. said, taking control of the situation. He glanced back at the BEAR-COM, and Spencer couldn't help but think that the Head of the Bear Guard looked impressed.

"Yes, B.D.," Evarita called. "Can someone read me the number?"

"Go ahead, Spencer," Professor Weaver said. "This is Evarita's area of expertise."

"License plates?" That seemed pretty weird.

"Background checks," B.D. corrected.

"Go ahead, dear," Bunny urged Spencer.

"Oh . . . uh . . . right," Spencer stammered, wishing he could stop everything and hug Bunny just for calling him "dear" again. He cleared his throat and read the license plate number slowly: "M-0-8-8-0-N-F."

"And the state?" she asked.

"Florida."

"All right, let's see what we're dealing with here . . ." Evarita leaned into her computer.

The room fell silent as everyone watched her typing furiously. After a few minutes, she returned her attention to the council meeting. Evarita sat back in her chair. Spencer knew Evarita well enough to tell from her grim expression that whatever they were dealing with was bad. Really bad.

20

"The van is registered to Moon Farm."

Bunny let out a pained growl and Pinky covered her eyes with her hot pink claws. "No, it can't be," she groaned.

Spencer and Aldo exchanged a look. *Moon Farm?*

"Have you rescued bears from Moon Farm before?" Spencer asked. He hoped the answer was yes. It would make things a whole lot easier. But something about the council's reaction gave Spencer a feeling the answer wasn't going to be what he hoped.

"We attempted a rescue at Moon Farm once before," B.D. said.

"Pinky lost her daughter to Moon Farm," Mr. Bee explained.

"What *is* Moon Farm?" Spencer asked, though now he was afraid to hear the answer.

"It's a toy factory," Mr. Bee began.

What can be so bad about a toy factory?

"Don't candy-coat it for the boy," Yude snarled. "That *toy factory* is just a front—a ridiculous stuffed animal business to cover what really goes on at that horrible and illegal place. Moon Farm is the site of the country's biggest bear smuggling operation. Bears are kidnapped and taken to Moon Farm where they wait, in chains or in cages, to be sold into some new torturous situation. If they live long enough to make it out at all."

Pinky whimpered.

"For goodness sake, Yude. Of all bears, you could show some sensitivity!" Mr. Bee glared at the green-cloaked bear. Bunny groaned miserably, but Spencer still didn't understand. *Bear smuggling?*

"The truth isn't always—"

"Not now, Yude," B.D. snapped.

"Sorry, but what is bear smuggling?" Spencer asked.

"It's black market bear trading—or bear-part trading, in the worst-case scenario," B.D. answered gruffly. Spencer stared at the Head of the Bear Guard in confusion. "Every year, thousands of bears are sold and traded on the black market. They are either captured from forests across the country or are sold by previous unsavory owners—backyard breeders, roadside menagerie owners, and two-bit carnival operators like Jay Grady. Moon Farm is a hub for these sorts of sales. At Moon Farm, the live bears are kept in dismal conditions and suffer all manner of unfair treatment. Once they leave Moon Farm, there's no record of their sale. A bear can disappear without a trace."

"Zoe wasn't that lucky, though . . ." Pinky said. Her BEAR-COM translated the sadness and anger in her voice. She and Spencer locked eyes. "Before your parents rescued me, my cub and I were owned by an exotic animal collector named Horrace Steele. He and his wife had two other bears and three lions. Our conditions were bad, but not like what some of the other rescued bears who came to Bearhaven lived through. At least they fed us, and they didn't remove or file down our teeth or claws . . . The Steeles sold Zoe to Moon Farm only months before your parents came to save us. They'd been selling their collection slowly; I could have ended up at Moon Farm myself. I wish . . ." Pinky stopped talking, like the memory had suddenly become too painful.

"You don't have to go on, Pinky," Mr. Bee said gently. "B.D. can explain the rest to Spencer another time if it's too difficult."

"No, I want to tell him. I can." Pinky looked back at Spencer. "Zoe was my only cub. She was even younger than Kate when she was sold to Moon Farm. When your parents rescued me I told them everything I possibly could to help them locate Zoe. They organized a rescue mission to Moon Farm as quickly as they could, but by the time they arrived . . ." Pinky paused. Spencer reached into his pocket. His hand was shaking as he clutched the jade bear. "She'd been at Moon Farm for four months when Bearhaven's team got there. At least . . . she'd been sold to Moon Farm four months earlier." Pinky shook her head. She looked to B.D.

"We don't know for certain what happened to Zoe once she got to Moon Farm because we don't know how their trading system works," B.D. said, taking over for Pinky. "But by the time we got there Zoe was gone."

"Gone?" Spencer managed to say.

"Zoe was sold, but she wasn't sold alive." B.D. answered. His voice was grim. Spencer could tell the bear was trying to be as sensitive as possible to Pinky. "The other bears were able to tell us that much."

"I don't . . . I don't understand . . ." Spencer stammered. He tried to make sense of what B.D. had just said but couldn't. "Why would anyone want to buy a bear that isn't . . ."

"Alive?" Aldo offered. "Why would *humans* want to do any of the torturous things they do to us?"

Yude jumped in. "If you stopped causing so much trouble and took a look around Bearhaven, Spencer Plain, you'd see that your kind have done *far* more harm than good." Spencer stared at the bear in shock.

"The Plains can hardly be lumped in with the rest of their species," Grandmama Grizabelle spoke up. "I think they've done quite a bit more good than harm, actually. *All* of them."

B.D. cut in to answer Spencer's question before anyone could say anything else. Spencer clutched the jade bear more tightly with every word B.D. said. "Unfortunately, some *parts* of bears are more valuable than live bears, Spencer. Everything from a bear's hide, to our paws, and even organs can be sold on the black market for a very high price." B.D. glanced in Pinky's direction to see whether she was all right before he continued. Pinky's head was bowed, but she didn't ask him to stop. The Head of the Guard went on. "Some bear parts are used in traditional medicines, others are decorative."

"There's even such an atrocious thing as bear paw soup," Raymond said.

Bear paw soup?! Animal-part trading was even worse than Spencer could have imagined. He thought he might throw up. It was the most horrible thing he'd ever heard. Poor

Zoe! And Pinky! That any of those things might happen to Kate . . . or could *be* happening to Kate right now was almost too much for him.

"They can't . . ." Spencer couldn't even finish the sentence. It was too terrifying to even say Kate's name out loud after that explanation. Professor Weaver seemed to understand without Spencer having to say any more.

"We're going to get to Kate before anything happens to her," Professor Weaver said, his voice quiet but determined.

B.D. rose up onto his hind legs, demanding everyone's attention. "We need to prepare for a rescue *now*. Kate's life is in immediate danger. We already know the location of Moon Farm, so we can mobilize right away. Evarita, are you prepared to travel?"

"Yes, of course," Evarita answered.

"Good. Make arrangements. I need you on location near Moon Farm by nine o'clock tonight so you can scout the facilities and handle the team's transportation. There's a TUBE station an hour or so from Moon Farm," B.D. went on. "We'll meet you there tomorrow evening. Professor Weaver, you'll be included in this mission. If Kate's health or safety come into question before her rescue, we'll want you there to make the call as her father."

"Absolutely." The Professor nodded.

"I'll stay here." Bunny's voice was grim. "I don't trust myself . . . if anything happened to Kate, I'd—"

"I won't have a mother bear on a mission this risky." B.D.'s voice was firm. "Your protective instincts are too unpredictable."

"Besides, one of us should stay here with the rest of the family. Winston, Jo-Jo, and Lisle need you, too," Professor Weaver reassured Bunny.

"B.D., I'd like to go, too." Aldo stepped up to the table. "I need to help find my sister."

"And me," Spencer added. He'd gotten Kate into this, he was going to do whatever it took to get her out.

"Spencer, we have clear orders from your parents to keep you safe in Bearhaven until their return," Professor Weaver said. Spencer opened his mouth to protest, but Evarita cut in.

"Actually, I'm a little concerned about being the only human operative on this mission, B.D. . . . I can't believe I am saying this because I know how important it is to keep Spencer safe." She hesitated, looking straight at Spencer. *Tell them I should go!* Spencer wanted to yell. With Mom, Dad, and Uncle Mark all out of communication, Evarita was the closest thing he had to family. If she said he could go, maybe the bears would be convinced it was all right to send him. "For Kate's sake, it might be a good idea to let Spencer come as a second human operative."

Yes!

"Aldo, if you're included in this mission, you'll be under special orders to watch out for Spencer," B.D. said gruffly. "Do you understand?"

"I understand," Aldo answered.

"Spencer, you'll be Evarita's reinforcement on this mission. Aldo, you'll protect Spencer." B.D. nodded, and with that, it was settled. Spencer was going on the mission to save Kate.

"Yude, you'll be our strategist," B.D. continued.

"I was planning on it." Yude pushed the hood of his cloak back so everyone in the room could see his eyes. They flashed from B.D. to Spencer, where they stayed. "We aren't losing another one of our cubs to humans."

Spencer looked away.

"Professor Weaver, Aldo, Spencer, and Yude, we leave at ten o'clock tonight," B.D. announced. "Evarita, we'll meet you at the Florida coast TUBE station at seven o'clock tomorrow night." B.D. lifted a claw to his BEAR-COM and switched it off. *"Abragan,"* he growled, then gave an authoritative nod.

"For the bears," everyone in the council room replied together. Hearing the word for the first time, Spencer echoed quietly: *"Abragan." For the bears.*

21

The elevator doors slid open to reveal the TUBE station. The tinted windows of the sleek white train were gleaming, like someone had spent the last hour shining the copper-colored glass. Spencer had to stop himself from sprinting across the platform and onto the train. He didn't want to seem too excited. Instead, he calmly stepped out of the elevator and looked over the TUBE, just like he thought an experienced operative reporting for duty would.

"I would imagine B.D. and Yude are already here somewhere," Professor Weaver said, stepping out from behind Spencer and swinging his head from side to side. "But I'll go see." The bear took off toward the first car of the train, where two members of the guard were running a security check.

Aldo came to stand beside Spencer. "Last time I was on the TUBE, I was the guard member making the security check. I didn't expect to go from checking the train to riding it so soon."

"Last time I was on the TUBE, I had to hide in a cardboard box to even make it out of the station," Spencer replied. "At least this time I'm on the team from the beginning." He noticed Aldo was chewing on something. "What are you eating anyway? It smells . . . spicy."

"Ginger root," Aldo answered, sending a puff of the sweet and spicy scent right into Spencer's face.

"Gross!" Spencer waved the bear's breath away.

"It doesn't taste much better than it smells," Aldo shrugged. "But Pinky told me ginger root eases pain. And it does make my teeth feel better."

"What's wrong with your teeth?" Spencer tried to peer into Aldo's mouth. The bear sealed his lips together, hiding his fangs.

"Just another toothache," he growled after a few seconds. "The honey's sweet enough to be worth a little tooth pain, though." Aldo added. He licked his lips theatrically.

Spencer laughed. If he loved honey half as much as Aldo did, he'd probably have a toothache, too, and plenty of cavities.

B.D. and Professor Weaver emerged from the front car of the TUBE, deep in conversation. Spencer and Aldo straightened up as the older bears approached.

"Aldo, Spencer, we'll start the briefing soon," Professor Weaver said, before stepping onto the passenger car himself. "Time to board the train, operatives."

Spencer and Aldo hurried across the platform. Boarding the TUBE, Spencer was impressed all over again by how cool the passenger car was. He especially liked the seats shaped like nautilus shells. The segmented hood on top of each seat could be pulled down to seal a passenger inside a reclined, pearly cocoon.

Yude's green cloak was draped over the side of one of the seats, and Spencer chose to sit as far from the sour bear as possible. He sank into his own cozy shell just as B.D. slid the door at the front of the passenger car open. "We'll be moving in the next five minutes." He glanced out the window. "But we might as well begin the briefing." He disappeared back into the car he had just come from. Spencer, Aldo, Yude, and Professor Weaver left their chosen seats to follow him into the dining room.

Raymond was at the front of the dining area, circling around a tower of boxes. Each box was marked with the image of a chef's hat. "This is all of it, B.D.," the chef bear said when the team of operatives entered the car.

"Were you able to include any salmon nuggets, Raymond?" Professor Weaver asked. "For the return trip?"

Spencer eyed the boxes of Raymond's meals. He hoped there were some salmon nuggets in there. Salmon nuggets were Kate's favorite food. He knew how happy they'd make her. Obviously, Professor Weaver knew, too.

"There are more salmon nuggets in those boxes than a single cub could eat in a week," Raymond answered. "But I'd better get off this train before you pull out of here." The bear lifted a claw to his chef's hat in a gesture that looked something like a salute, and headed for the door.

"Thank you," Professor Weaver called after the chef.

As soon as everyone was seated facing B.D., the bear began. "At seven o'clock tomorrow night we will arrive at the TUBE station in Florida. We'll be met by Evarita, who has already arrived. She's scouting the site now, testing how we can enter Moon Farm undetected, and arranging our transportation from the TUBE station. Yude, she will be in communication with you regarding strategy."

"Of course." Yude's voice was stronger and more enthusiastic than Spencer had ever heard it. *Strategy must be Yude's specialty.*

"This is an overnight mission," B.D. continued. "We'll go in after dark and be out of Moon Farm before dawn. The focus of this mission is not to try to stop all of Moon Farm's operations. We are there to get Kate out. We'll review the specific details of the mission once Evarita and Yude have been able to communicate. They will download to us what Evarita scouted tonight and combine it with Yude's prior knowledge of the Moon Farm floor plan.

"But here's what we already know: Each Moon Farm product is marked with a gold foil tag in the shape of a bear." B.D. held up a teddy bear with a shiny tag attached to its ear. "Each bear operative going into Moon Farm will have one of these tags attached to their ear. All BEAR-COMs will be left on the TUBE. We'll be using Ear-COMs for this mission." Spencer and Aldo exchanged a look. As scary as this mission was starting to sound, Spencer couldn't help but feel excited. He'd get to use one of the bears' cooler pieces of equipment for the first time. "Spencer." B.D. interrupted Spencer's thoughts. For a second, Spencer thought he was about to get in trouble for letting his mind wander. "Professor Weaver has to put the finishing touches on your Ear-COM tonight, but you will have one by the time we arrive."

"I'm reprogramming one of your mother's Ear-COM's for you, and making it a bit smaller, of course," Professor Weaver explained.

"Thanks!" Spencer could hardly believe it. He was getting his own high-tech, bear-made operative equipment. Well, almost his own . . . but that it was once Mom's made it even more awesome. Spencer imagined himself on a rescue mission with Mom and Dad—three Plain operatives working together, communicating through Ear-COMs . . . He stopped himself. Before he could go out on bear rescue missions with Mom and Dad, Mom and Dad had to make it back to Bearhaven. Spencer gave his jade bear a quick squeeze. Hopefully, wherever Uncle Mark was, he was getting closer to bringing Mom and Dad home. He had to be.

"Ear-COMs work similarly to BEAR-COMs," the professor continued. "They translate Ragayo to human language, and vice versa. The Ear-COM is intended to be a more covert device than the BEAR-COM, so it's much smaller and fits directly into your ear. In order for your words to be heard by another member of this team, you must first say their name. When you say another operative's name, your Ear-COMs will connect and your words will transmit directly into the ear of your teammate. Of course, if you say multiple names, your Ear-COM will connect with multiple operatives. And finally, to connect to the Ear-COMs of all the operatives on this mission, say 'team.' In order to disconnect your Ear-COM, say 'disconnect.' It's as simple as that." The professor looked to B.D.

"Thank you, Professor. Aldo and Spencer, you are the only operatives who don't have experience with the Ear-COMs. If you have any additional questions, please speak with Professor Weaver after the briefing."

Can I keep it? was the only question Spencer could think of. He'd be sure to ask Professor Weaver later.

"The final order of business this evening," B.D. continued, "is mission packs."

Mission packs? Spencer had no idea what those were, but they sounded awesome. He hoped there was one for him.

The door behind B.D. opened and Marguerite, the TUBE's attendant, stepped into the car. The large, dark brown bear was wearing her blue cap and matching blue vest with gold trim. Her honey-colored muzzle was stretched into a wide smile, and she pushed a rolling cart into the car ahead of her.

" 'Mission packs' was my cue to enter," she said brightly, winking at Spencer. "I'll leave these with you, B.D."

"Thank you, Marguerite." B.D. took the cart.

"Once you're through with the briefing I'll come around with tea and a bite to eat," Marguerite said, then left the way she'd come.

"You will each carry a mission pack tomorrow night," B.D. said, picking up where he'd left off. "They're filled with tools and emergency supplies you may need." Yude, Professor Weaver, and Aldo padded up to the cart. Spencer followed, watching as B.D. passed the bears their mission packs. Each pack was covered in fur that matched the bear who was supposed to wear it. When the bears slipped their head and one leg through the loop, they looked as if they were putting on a messenger bag. Once the mission pack was on, it practically disappeared because it blended so well with the bear's fur. It just looked as though each of the bears had gotten a little lumpier on one side.

Maybe I don't want a mission pack, Spencer thought. *It will look like there's a koala riding on my back!*

To Spencer's relief, when B.D. retrieved Spencer's mission pack from the cart, it wasn't furry like the others. It was just a regular black backpack.

"Thanks." Spencer took the backpack and returned to his seat.

"All right, operatives." B.D. stood back on his hind legs. "Familiarize yourselves with the contents of your mission packs and get some rest. We have a long ride ahead and you all need to be sharp if—when—we're going to get Kate out of Moon Farm tomorrow night."

22

Spencer stepped into the wardrobe car with his mission pack slung over one shoulder. He couldn't wait to open it and see what was inside.

The wardrobe car was empty, just like Spencer expected. Only human operatives ever came in here. The bears had no reason to. After all, there wasn't much anyone could do to make a bear look like anything other than a bear. Mom, Dad, Uncle Mark, and Evarita, on the other hand, could hide their identities behind all kinds of disguises.

Full-length mirrors lined the sides of the car, and on either end there was a big closet, one for women, the other for men. The door to the women's closet stood open. Spencer could see shelves full of wigs in every length and color, and beside them, a chest of drawers filled with the prosthetics the human operatives used to completely change their appearances. The chest looked just like the one Uncle Mark had shown him in the men's closet the last time Spencer was on the TUBE.

The last time Spencer saw Mom, he hadn't recognized her. Not at first. She'd been totally transformed by prosthetics. It had been an accident he'd seen her at all, but on the last rescue mission—getting Ro Ro and her cubs away from Jay Grady's—Spencer had stumbled into a room where Margo Lalicki was having a video conference call with her boss, Pam. Spencer had been in the room with Margo, on Margo's side of the call, and Mom had been on the screen, right next to Pam.

Spencer shuddered. Just thinking about Pam's long nails that curled in an imitation of bear claws made the hair stand up on Spencer's arms. That man was *creepy*. And seeing Mom waiting on him—even if she was undercover, and just pretending to be a maid—made Spencer's stomach twist into angry knots.

Spencer turned to leave the women's closet. Shelves filled with shoes stretched from floor to ceiling on either side of the door. One of the shelves caught Spencer's eye. Instead of shoes it was filled with framed photographs. Spencer took a step closer. In one picture, Mom and Dad were both dressed as police officers. They stood on either side of a silver-colored bear. *Wait* . . . Spencer looked more closely. The bear between Mom and Dad was Bunny! It must have been taken on the way back from her rescue mission.

Spencer scanned a few more pictures. Mom and Dad were in almost all of them, and Uncle Mark was in some. Spencer looked at the faces of all the bears on their first trips to Bearhaven. He recognized several of the bears, and each picture made him more and more proud of Mom and Dad. They'd saved so many bears, giving so many animals better lives.

Spencer spotted a picture a little farther back on the shelf. He pushed the other frames aside, eager to get a closer

look. It was different from the others. Mom and Dad weren't in disguises, and they weren't on a return trip. They were in Bearhaven—Spencer could see the Lab right behind them—and there wasn't a bear standing between them, but a little boy.

Spencer squinted at the picture. He picked it up and stared at the boy's face. There was no question, the boy was Spencer. But that didn't make any sense! Spencer had never been to Bearhaven before Mom and Dad disappeared and Uncle Mark brought him there a little over two weeks ago. Had he?

"Then how . . ." Spencer whispered. *Wait.* He suddenly remembered the very first thing Bunny said to him when he arrived in Bearhaven. She'd hugged him and said: "We haven't seen you in so long." At the time, her remark hadn't registered. Spencer had still been in shock, barely used to the idea that bears were actually *talking* to him, let alone welcoming him to their home.

Suddenly, he heard a bear huff.

"More meddling?" a BEAR-COM translated. Spencer was so startled he dropped the picture frame. The glass shattered when it hit the floor. Spencer looked down at the photo of his family, now surrounded by broken glass, thanks to Yude. Spencer grit his teeth, frustrated. "And more destruction," Yude added. That was the last straw. Spencer was suddenly furious. He stormed out of the closet.

"WHAT DID I EVER DO TO YOU?!" he yelled. Yude was sitting back on his haunches in the middle of the wardrobe car, his smug expression reflected over and over again by the mirrors that lined the sides of the car. "Why do you have to be so nasty all the time?!" Spencer's hands were balled into fists, and the satisfied look on Yude's face was only making Spencer even angrier. "I GET IT, okay?! My parents didn't rescue you. You don't owe humans anything. You're some kind of genius for finding Bearhaven on your own. Congratulations! You don't need me or my family, so why don't you just LEAVE. ME. ALONE!"

"You don't *get* anything, Spencer," Yude growled threateningly. He made a popping sound with his jaw. "You're a spoiled child with no idea about the consequences of your own actions. Kate isn't the only bear whose life you've damaged." *Pop.*

Spencer took a step back. What did Yude mean? He didn't know the consequences of his own actions? Kate wasn't the only bear . . . ?

Pop! Yude's eyes were locked on Spencer.

Spencer took another step back. He knew that sound. Jaw popping was a warning. It was one of the ways bears in the wild showed they were angry, and if whatever was making them angry didn't stop, it meant the bear could become aggressive and attack.

Spencer knew better than to fight with Yude right now. Mom and Dad always said interactions between humans and bears went badly only because of misunderstandings. If humans understood bear behavior better, and bears understood human behavior better, they'd know how to react to each other's signals. If they could just communicate, so many lives—human and bear—wouldn't be lost. Yet here

Spencer was, listening to Yude's jaw pop and recognizing all the signs that Yude was getting angrier and not backing down. He couldn't help himself.

"I think you're just a grumpy, old, human-hating bear," Spencer shot back through gritted teeth.

23

Yude snarled. He took two quick paces toward Spencer, his teeth flashing way too close to Spencer's face. Spencer opened his mouth to scream but nothing came out. Yude stepped even closer and gave a deep growl. Then it happened.

The images that always made Spencer panic when he climbed ropes in gym class back home or trees in Bearhaven hit him all at once. But for the first time, the images came in order, creating a complete, terrifying memory.

Spencer saw Yude's face up close to his own. The bear grabbed Spencer, whose head knocked against the metal BEAR-COM around Yude's neck. Then Spencer's head started to bleed. Yude grabbed Spencer and carried him—roughly—up into a tall tree. Mom and Dad were screaming up to them from the ground below. Spencer thrashed against Yude, who carried him higher and higher. Then suddenly Yude wasn't carrying him anymore. Spencer was falling, and fast. He crashed through branches and leaves as he careened toward the ground.

"AHHHHH!!!" A scream tore out of Spencer's throat, and he realized his eyes were squeezed shut. He forced himself to open them.

"And you wonder why I don't like humans," Yude growled. "What's the matter with you?"

The bear was sitting back on his haunches. There was no sign of the jaw popping Spencer had heard before—Yude looked calm and unamused.

"What happened the first time I came to Bearhaven?" Spencer demanded. "Why did you try to kill me?"

"If I'd wanted to kill you, trust me, you wouldn't be standing here right now, so be careful what you accuse me of," Yude snapped. "You don't remember what happened?"

Spencer shook his head, bracing himself for whatever Yude had to say.

"Well, then. That changes things," Yude began. "You came to Bearhaven for the first time just after I arrived there myself." His tone was matter-of-fact, as though he was reciting food choices on Raymond's menu. He drew his green cloak tighter around himself and continued, not looking at Spencer. "I'm not proud of what happened, but recovering from the kind of abuse I suffered was not easy for me. Many of Bearhaven's bears have suffered at the hands of humans, and recovery is difficult, and different, for each of us.

"I escaped a circus where things were . . . terrible. I was still adjusting when you and your family came to visit. Being around humans was still hard for me. Even though I knew about your family's work and involvement in creating Bearhaven, it brought back a lot of pain and anger and confusion to see humans in a place where I was just starting to feel safe." Yude glanced at Spencer. Spencer stayed silent, his hand wrapped around the jade bear in his pocket.

"You were very young. I don't know human years well enough to say exactly how old, but you were much smaller than you are now. Your parents were walking you through Bearhaven when they stopped to watch a group of Bear Guard recruits practicing tree climbing. I was one of the recruits. It was one of my first days of training but I was already determined to be the Head of the Guard one day." Yude's voice got quieter, and for the first time, Spencer could hear some emotion in it. "I wanted to protect the one place that had started to feel like home to me. Somehow, you got close enough to grab a fistful of my fur. You yanked on it and I reacted without thinking. Everything was clouded by my experience in the circus. I panicked. I grabbed you and climbed up into a tree. You were obviously afraid—so was I—and you squirmed out of my grasp and fell."

Adrenaline pounded through Spencer's veins. He could practically feel himself falling all over again.

"It was all an unfortunate accident," Yude growled. "Your parents never brought you to Bearhaven with them after that. They said it was unsafe for a small child, though everyone knew they really thought it was only *I* who was unsafe. I was removed from Bear Guard training for 'instability,' which meant—"

"You could never be Head of the Guard," Spencer finished Yude's sentence. "I . . . had no idea." He wanted to be mad at the bear. Yude was the reason Mom and Dad had never told him about Bearhaven. Plus, Yude was the reason Spencer had a fear of falling he'd never been able to explain until today. Still, he understood. Whatever he'd done as a little kid had

made something in Yude snap. Spencer had been acting like a curious human kid, and Yude had reacted like a bear whose only experience with humans was torture.

"I wasn't aware that you didn't remember that incident, or that you hadn't been told," Yude added. Spencer shook his head, still trying to collect his thoughts.

No matter what had happened between himself and Yude in the past, right now they were on the same team, and tomorrow night they were going to save Kate. They had to.

"Yude," Spencer cleared his throat. He could hardly believe what he was about to do. "How do you say 'I'm sorry' in Ragayo?"

Yude didn't answer for a long moment. He looked Spencer over, then lifted a claw to switch off his BEAR-COM. *"Acha kunchaich,"* he growled, then turned the BEAR-COM back on. "We use it as an apology," Yude said. "But it means, 'I didn't know my own strength.'"

"Acha kunchaich," Spencer repeated.

The bear nodded gravely, then turned and padded quietly out of the wardrobe car. His green cloak hid most of his body from sight as he left.

Spencer looked out into the dark tunnel of the TUBE. *"Kate isn't the only bear whose life you've damaged,"* Yude had said. Even though Spencer and Yude had put the past behind them, the bear's words still stung.

"We have to get to Kate before anything happens to her," Spencer whispered. He watched the copper-colored window whip past signal lights. The TUBE was flying through the tunnel, but Spencer didn't think it could possibly go fast enough.

24

Spencer hopped off the TUBE and onto the station platform in Florida. The station looked identical to the one in Bearhaven, but it was hotter here, much hotter. Spencer wiped a bead of sweat from his forehead. He had his mission pack slung over one shoulder and a few pages of scrawled notes folded in his pocket. He'd enlisted Aldo's help that morning to reconstruct as much of the STORM journal as they could on a piece of scrap paper. He'd wanted to review his operative training before the mission, and he'd spent the rest of the TUBE ride doing just that. Now he was ready. Whatever happened at Moon Farm, he'd handle it like an operative.

"Spencer," a voice rang in Spencer's ear. It was Aldo. "Was there any honey in your mission pack?" the bear asked. Spencer lifted a hand to his ear, carefully adjusting the volume on his Ear-COM the way Professor Weaver had shown him. He was still getting used to wearing the translating device. It felt as if someone had filled his ear with clay. Even so, Spencer had never felt so cool.

"Why would there be honey?" Spencer answered. He knew his Ear-COM would transmit the words right into

Aldo's ear now that their devices were connected, but he couldn't imagine what good honey would do them on the rescue mission.

Aldo lumbered off the TUBE. His BEAR-COM and silver cuffs were gone, and there was a gold foil bear tag attached to one of his ears.

"There's a Raymond's fuel bar in mine," he said when he reached Spencer. "But those things could always use a little bit of honey if you ask me."

"Nope, no honey. Sorry," Spencer answered. "And I think if we're in enough trouble that we need to eat our emergency food supply, we're probably not going to be too worried about how sweet it is."

"That's what you think." Aldo's tone was playful but forced, like he was trying to keep them both from getting too nervous about the mission. "You've never *had* a Raymond's fuel bar. Disconnect." The bear cut the connection between his Ear-COM and Spencer's.

Spencer laughed and rushed to catch up with B.D., Yude, and Professor Weaver, who were stepping into an elevator on the far side of the platform.

"B.D.," Spencer called. "What about my clothes?" He looked down at the jeans and plain gray T-shirt he'd worn out of Bearhaven twenty-one hours ago. "Should I change into some kind of disguise?"

"Evarita will handle your wardrobe," B.D. answered. "Human clothing isn't exactly my strong suit. Disconnect."

The Head of the Guard hit a button in the elevator once all the bears and Spencer were packed inside. The doors slid shut. Not a minute later, they slid open again, revealing a cluster of palm trees outside. Spencer moved to leave the elevator right away, but B.D. stopped him.

"Team," Evarita said from somewhere nearby, connecting all the Ear-COMs at once. "All clear." B.D. moved aside, letting Spencer out of the elevator. He spotted Evarita right away. She was off to the left, leaning up against a big ice cream truck on a dirt road a few yards away.

"Chipwich or Choco Taco?" she called. Spencer ran over to her.

"Is that a uniform?" he asked. Evarita was wearing blue pants, a button-down short-sleeved shirt, and a blue baseball cap. An outline of a bear was printed in white on the front of the baseball cap. It matched the foil tag on each of the Bearhaven bear operatives' ears. The letters *M.F.* were embroidered in gold on the pocket of the shirt.

"A Moon Farm factory uniform, actually. I have one for you in the front of the truck. B.D., you four should get out of sight," Evarita hurried on. "There's more traffic on this road than I'd expected." She swung open the back doors of the truck. Spencer poked his head inside to look into the big empty space. *No ice cream.* Aldo hurried past him and climbed aboard. Yude climbed into the truck next, then Professor Weaver and B.D. With the four very large bears in the truck, there was hardly any space left.

"You're riding up front with me," Evarita said to Spencer as she shut the doors, hiding the bears. "Hurry up and change. I'll stay here until you're ready."

Spencer rushed up to the front of the truck and opened the passenger-side door. A uniform just like the one Evarita was wearing was folded up on the seat. He climbed in and changed as quickly as he could. Once he'd transferred his jade bear from the pocket of his jeans into the factory uniform pants, he shoved his regular clothing underneath the passenger seat. "All right!" he called as he pulled the blue cap down on his head. A second later, Evarita opened the driver-side door and slid in behind the wheel.

"You look ready for a mission, Spencer." Evarita started the truck. "Team, can everyone hear me in the back?" she asked.

"We can hear you, Evarita," B.D. answered. "Can you give us the update?"

Evarita pulled onto the dirt road and made a quick U-turn that was met with a chorus of grunts and growls from the back of the truck. "Sorry!" she called to the bears.

"All right," she began. "Yude and I have spoken about strategy, and we've determined that since we have both bears and humans on our team, getting into Moon Farm may actually, ironically, be the easiest part of this rescue mission. The place is filled to the brim with stuffed animals, some of them bigger than you, B.D. We're going to use that to our advantage." Some of Spencer's nervousness faded away. Everything seemed to be under control.

"The last shift in the factory gets off at nine o'clock p.m. At eight-fifty, Spencer and I are going to wheel three of you bears in on metal carts. You all have the gold tags on your ears already, just like the ones Moon Farm uses to mark their products. If you stay completely still, you'll pass as stuffed animals, and if anyone asks, we'll tell them you're part of a late shipment. I doubt anyone will ask, though, not at nine o'clock at night. The workers want to get out of the factory and home as soon as their shifts are over.

"Spencer and I will each bring one of you, then I'll double back for the third bear. Timing may get a little tricky, so we'll have to move fast. Once the warehouse door closes for the night, it's alarmed. There won't be any getting in after that, so we all need to be in the warehouse and hidden by the time the last workers leave.

"Once we're inside, we'll need to locate Kate as quickly as possible. Yude's knowledge of Moon Farm's floor plan from the last rescue attempt has given us a good indication of where to start; the layout seems to be the same. The building is divided into two halves. The part that's accessible to the cargo dock where we'll be arriving is the factory section, where the toy business—the legal side of Moon Farm's business—all happens. That toy business is the cover for the illegal bear smuggling. It's the other half of the building we'll have to cross over to where all the illegal operations take place.

"Once we've gained access to the smuggling section of the building, Aldo, your sense of smell will be necessary as we search for Kate. Professor Weaver, since you're most comfortable using the mechanical hand, Yude thought it would be best if you were the one to stay with the boat. You'll need to get it out of sight, then bring it back for the getaway when necessary."

Boat? What boat?

"Of course," Professor Weaver agreed.

"Any questions?"

"I have a question," Spencer said after a pause. "What boat?"

"Nobody mentioned it?" Evarita sounded surprised. "Moon Farm is an island. Makes things a bit more complicated, huh?"

Spencer didn't answer. He looked straight ahead as they merged onto a highway. The coast spread out alongside it, and the waves crashed against the shore. *An island?* He was starting to see why everyone kept calling this mission risky.

25

Evarita opened the back doors of the ice cream truck and stepped aside.

The campsite parking lot she'd pulled into was empty except for a single motorcycle parked on the far side of the lot, but the motorcycle's rider was nowhere in sight. With the low-hanging branches of a few trees concealing the whole back half of the truck, the coast was clear.

"Team, come on out," she said to the bears, who looked more than ready to leave the cramped ice cream truck behind. "The boat isn't far, but we should move quickly."

The bears leaped down from the back of the truck one by one and hurried into the trees as Evarita locked up the truck.

"Lead the way, Evarita," B.D. said. Spencer couldn't see the bear, but B.D.'s voice came through loud and clear in his Ear-COM. "We'll follow out of sight."

"All right, this way." She took off at a jog toward a hiking trail that led from the parking lot into the trees, and Spencer followed. He glanced into the trees as he ran, looking for the rest of Bearhaven's team. Every once in a while, he caught a flash of fur or heard a twig snap, but mostly it seemed as though he and Evarita were completely alone.

The hiking trail ended at a small, rocky beach. It was abandoned except for a rickety-looking dock with a big, flashy, white speedboat parked beside it. The boat was bigger than Spencer had expected. He guessed it could hold at least twenty people, or maybe ten people and a few large bears. A small cabin for the driver sat in the middle of the boat, and an awning-covered seating area took up the back half.

One by one, the bears emerged from the trees and sprinted across the beach ahead of Evarita and Spencer, kicking up sand and pebbles as they ran. They tore across the dock, which creaked beneath them, then hurtled aboard the boat.

By the time Spencer and Evarita jumped aboard, the boat had stopped rocking dangerously from the impact of the bears, and B.D., Professor Weaver, Yude, and Aldo lay motionless and silent in a heap. If it weren't for their heavy breathing and the movements of their eyes, Spencer was sure they'd pass for four oversized stuffed toy animals.

"Can you untie us from the dock, Spencer?" Evarita called, heading for the driver's cabin. "Be careful though, those wooden planks were treacherous *before* four bears thundered over them."

"Sure." Spencer stepped back onto the dock, which quaked beneath his weight. He'd better make this quick. He rushed to the back of the boat and released the rope from the metal cleat it was tied to, then untied the rope at the front and tossed it into the boat. He stepped aboard, then grabbed the fenders, the rubber bumpers that kept the side of the speedboat from scraping against the dock, and pulled them in after himself.

Spencer went to join Evarita in the cabin. He looked around at the shiny wood paneling and the white leather driver's seat. Before he could ask where she'd gotten the boat, its engine roared to life.

"Let's get this show on the road, shall we?" Evarita said. She handed him a life vest that matched the one she'd buckled around herself. "We have a late shipment of very large, very important stuffed animals to deliver. Hold on to something while we're moving," she added.

Spencer scrambled to get his life vest on and buckled as Evarita backed the boat away from the dock. A second later, she pushed the throttle forward, sending them soaring out into open water. Spencer grabbed on to the windowsill beside him in the driver's cabin, steadying himself as the boat picked up speed.

As the boat sailed across the water, Spencer tried hard to calm his nerves. The faster they approached Moon Farm, the more anxious he was to see Kate. There was no telling how they'd find her or what it would take to get her out. Kate had helped him with each one of his STORM training exercises, but neither of them had ever expected he'd been training for the cub's own rescue. What if he wasn't ready? Spencer pushed the thought away. He was ready. He had to be.

"There it is," Yude's voice came through Spencer's Ear-COM, interrupting his thoughts.

Spencer looked up, bracing himself for his first glimpse of Moon Farm. An island loomed on the horizon. Cliffs rose up out of the water. On top of the cliffs, a solid cement wall extended high into the sky and seemed to surround the entire island. The eerie silhouette of a bear was painted in white on the cement wall, towering over the water. The bear silhouette was at least fifty feet tall.

Moon Farm looked like a terrifying prison. And Kate was locked inside.

26

Spencer jumped off the boat and onto a wide, sturdy dock at the base of one of Moon Farm's rocky cliff sides. They'd found the place where shipments were loaded and unloaded, but it was dark, and getting late. There was nobody else here, and aside from a small silver dingy tied farther up on the dock, there weren't any other boats.

Spencer unbuckled his life vest and tossed it back into the boat. He caught the rope Evarita tossed him and quickly wrapped it around a cleat in a secure figure-eight. B.D., Aldo, and Yude were slumped on the floor, still pretending to be a late shipment of huge stuffed bears. Professor Weaver had moved to the cabin just before they arrived, staying out of sight, then preparing to drive back to the abandoned dock until it was time for the getaway.

Evarita joined Spencer on the dock and strode over to a row of L-shaped metal carts. Each cart's flatbed was large enough for a bear to stretch out on top of it with his back propped against the handle. Evarita rolled the first cart over.

"Help me grab one of those stuffed bears, will ya?" she said, getting right into character as a Moon Farm worker.

"Uh . . . sure," Spencer replied. *How am I supposed to do that?*

"Just hold this thing steady," Evarita added, as if reading Spencer's mind. He took the cart handle and Evarita got back on the boat. She approached Yude and wrapped her arms around him. When she set him down on the cart, it looked as if she'd carried him there, but Spencer could tell the bear hadn't been carried at all. There was no way Evarita would have been able to lift him. Yude had walked, dragging his paws as he went. Spencer didn't think anyone who wasn't standing right there would be able to tell.

He hurried across the dock to grab a second cart. Evarita returned to the boat for Aldo, who mimicked Yude's performance, helping Evarita get him onto the cart and into position.

"I'll be back for the last one," Evarita called, as though she was really letting the boat driver know to wait. She grabbed the handles of Yude's cart and started to push. "Let's go."

Spencer braced himself against the handle of Aldo's cart and pushed with all his might. The cart flew forward! He'd expected pushing the cart to take all his strength, but Aldo must be lighter than he'd thought. He glanced down at Aldo, then up at Yude and Evarita, who were rolling steadily forward, and realized his miscalculation. Both Aldo and Yude had two of their legs flopped over the sides of their carts. *The bears are helping to push!*

"Hurry." He heard Evarita's voice in his ear.

Spencer started to push again. He and Aldo raced to catch up with Evarita and Yude just as they disappeared through the black iron gates into Moon Farm.

A small tunnel waited on the other side of the gates that opened into a stone courtyard. Across the courtyard, a huge gray building rose up into the night sky. The building spanned the entire width of the island, sandwiched between the cement outer wall on both sides.

A huge spotlit neon sign read *MOON FARM FACTORY*.

A minute later, the lights illuminating Moon Farm's sign blinked off. A door with the words *Employee Entrance* painted above it banged open, and people started to trickle out of the building. They were all dressed identically in blue pants, short-sleeved button-down shirts, and blue baseball caps. The white bear on their caps and the gold letters, *M.F,* on their shirts were becoming all too familiar. Just like Evarita predicted, the factory workers looked exhausted and more

than ready to go home as they trudged toward a tunnel farther down the cement wall.

"It's nine o'clock," Evarita whispered urgently as she strode across the courtyard, pushing Yude ahead of her. She headed straight for a big door the size of Spencer's garage at home. *Warehouse Entrance*, the white paint above the open door read. Spencer hurried along behind with Aldo.

He tried to ignore the workers who continued to trudge out of the employee exit, but he couldn't help looking over after every few steps to make sure nobody was coming toward them. Nobody even glanced in the Bearhaven team's direction. *The plan is working!*

Spencer rolled Aldo into the enormous warehouse and realized exactly why the plan was going to *keep* working. The cavernous room was lined with shelves that stretched from the cement floor to the ceiling, three stories up. Every shelf Spencer could see held row after row after row of stuffed animals. It was like stepping into a huge, towering, plush zoo. The largest, life-sized stuffed animals were on the bottom shelf: bears, crocodiles, and perfectly coiled, brightly colored snakes. The stuffed animals on the second shelf up were a little smaller, and the stuffed animals on the shelf above that one were smaller still. An array of different types of plush birds lined the whole left side of the aisle, their wings and beaks poking out every which way.

Evarita swung her cart to the right, and then into an aisle in the bear section. "You ready to head outta here, Ed?" a voice called from somewhere close by.

"Just about," another voice answered. "Doin' final check."

Spencer rushed to spin his cart into the aisle Evarita had chosen. She was there, hurrying Yude onto a bottom shelf, pushing aside a life-sized stuffed polar bear to make space.

"I gotta go back for that last bear," Evarita grumbled, signaling to B.D. over Ear-COM she was on her way back for him. "Hide," she added in a whisper to Spencer, then grabbed her empty cart and dashed back the way they'd come.

Aldo forced his way in between a black bear and a grizzly and disappeared into a sea of fake fur. The sound of heavy footsteps rang out in the next aisle over. Spencer dove in between two stuffed brown bears and moved as far back on the shelf as he could, burrowing deeper into the soft, oversized toys to hide. He stopped only when he hit something that grunted quietly. It was Aldo. Spencer stationed himself behind the bear to wait. His heart pounded in his chest. Nobody had told him what to do if he got caught. Running wasn't an option now that he was surrounded by huge stuffed bears.

The footsteps were getting louder. Spencer held his breath. He was terrified of making even the tiniest sound.

"Aw, man, someone left a cart again, and this shelf's a mess," a voice whined from a few feet away. *Oh no* . . . Some of the stuffed bears shifted around him. *The guy's rearranging the shelf!* Spencer realized with horror. "Makin' these things look more real every day," the voice muttered.

"Just leave it, Ed. Morning shift'll have to straighten it out. We're gonna miss the boat back to the mainland. C'mon."

"All right, all right," Ed called. The stuffed animals at the front of the shelf stopped rustling, and the sound of heavy footsteps picked up again. "Shut the big door, will ya?"

A loud metallic rattling sound filled the warehouse.

"They're shutting the door!" Spencer hissed, knowing the message would reach Evarita and B.D. "Where are you?!" He listened hard for an answer, but nothing came.

There was a thud and the rattling stopped. The warehouse's fluorescent lights snapped off. Spencer couldn't see a thing. He couldn't hear anything except for the quiet breathing of the two real bears hidden among the stuffed animals around him. Then Evarita's voice was in his ear.

"We didn't make it in."

27

"Nobody panic." Yude's voice came through Spencer's Ear-COM. But it was too late. Spencer was panicking. Evarita and B.D. were on the other side of the warehouse door. If they tried to get in now, an alarm would sound, they'd all get caught, and Kate would never even know they'd come for her. But without Evarita, Spencer would be the only human operative on this mission, and without B.D.—

"Yude," B.D. growled. "You're in charge." Spencer's stomach flopped. Putting the past behind them so they could work as a team to save Kate was one thing. Trusting Yude to *lead* the mission to save Kate was a different thing altogether.

"Evarita and I will stay with Professor Weaver," B.D. continued. "We'll prepare the escape route so that we're ready to get you three and Kate out of there. You can reach us by Ear-COM at any time." The bear fell silent, and for a second, Spencer had a horrible feeling that was the last they'd hear from B.D. and Evarita. He reached for his jade bear. Was the mission doomed? Was Kate going to end up just like Zoe after all?

"Team," B.D. finally said. "Just because this mission is not going according to plan doesn't mean it's over. You will get Kate out of there tonight." The bear fell silent, then after a moment, disconnected the full team communication.

"Aldo, Spencer," Yude said, taking over. His voice was confident, as if he led successful missions to Moon Farm every day. "Let's move."

Spencer was suddenly swept up in a big, furry avalanche as Yude and Aldo pushed through stuffed bears to get to the front of the shelf. Spencer tumbled out onto the darkened warehouse floor, then scrambled to his feet.

"I can't see anything." He tried to get his eyes to adjust to the dark, but it was no use. The darkness was so complete it was like being blindfolded.

"You don't need to see right now," Yude answered. "You just need to hold on."

"Hold on?"

"To Aldo," Yude explained. "For the climb to the roof."

Spencer gulped. "Climb?" he asked weakly. "To the *roof*?"

"As long as you hold on to Aldo, you won't be in any danger," Yude assured him. "Aldo, the climb is three stories up the metal shelves. They're bolted to the floor and ceiling. They're stable. I'll meet you at the top."

"Okay," Aldo answered. "I'm right beside you, Spencer. Climb on."

The last thing Spencer wanted to do in the pitch-black warehouse was climb onto Aldo's back. Going three stories up a set of metal shelves didn't sound at all danger-free to him, either, but he didn't have much choice. He was an operative and Yude was giving the orders.

Spencer reached an arm out in the dark and found Aldo. He climbed onto the bear's back.

"You okay up there, little man?" Aldo asked softly. *He can probably feel my hands shaking,* Spencer thought, embarrassed by how afraid he was.

"Yes. Let's go." He tried to sound as confident as Yude. He felt Aldo straighten up, walk a few paces, then rise onto his hind legs. The bear started to climb. The higher Aldo climbed up the metal shelves, the more difficult it became for Spencer to hold on.

"We are *way* too high off the ground," Spencer muttered through gritted teeth. His hands were sweating and images of himself falling flashed through his head, making his whole body freeze up. The only good thing about climbing higher was the closer they got to the roof, the more Spencer could see. Moonlight was shining in through a skylight.

"Almost there, little man," Aldo answered quietly as he continued to scale the three stories of shelves. A moment later, the bear grunted, then dropped to all fours on the highest shelf in the tower. He crouched down, giving Spencer the chance to slide off his back. Spencer landed on wobbly legs in a moonlit section of the metal shelf that had been cleared of toys. He could see Yude was already there, up on his hind legs, pushing against the glass skylight.

Spencer rushed over to the bears, searching for any way he might help open the skylight. *The sooner that skylight opens, the sooner we're off these shelves and on the roof.*

28

Yude grabbed Spencer's shirt in his teeth. Spencer felt himself swing up toward the open skylight and into Aldo's outstretched paw. The bear scooped him onto the roof and set him down carefully. A moment later, Yude scrambled out of the warehouse to join Spencer and Aldo in the moonlight.

Spencer looked down the long, wide roof. The far end seemed like it was a mile away. On top of the farthest section of roof, there was a stone tower. It reminded Spencer of a medieval castle, and it only made Moon Farm look even more threatening. "This building is huge," he whispered. He tried not to imagine how many bears were being kept in all this space or how long it might take them to find Kate.

"Yes, it is," Yude answered. "Which is why we need to move quickly. We'll go in through one of the skylights on the other half of the building. Come on." With that, the bear set off down the roof. Spencer and Aldo hurried to catch up.

When they reached the first skylight on the half of the building that housed Moon Farm's illegal operations, Yude, Aldo, and Spencer stopped running. Spencer stayed back a few paces, afraid of what he might see if he looked down into the building. Whatever was on the floor below them was still brightly lit, the light glowed up through the glass.

"Spencer, you have tools in your mission pack?" Yude asked.

"A hammer and a crowbar," Spencer answered. He slipped his pack off and unzipped it.

"Use the crowbar to get the skylight open," Yude directed, swinging his head toward the glowing glass.

Spencer pulled the tool out of his mission pack. He stepped up to the skylight and examined the window frame. "That's weird. It looks like someone just did this."

"Did what?" Aldo asked.

"Broke in with a crowbar. Look!" Spencer pointed to where the metal window frame was bent, and the section of scratched glass beside it. He didn't think Evarita would have gone so far as to pry open a skylight yesterday when she was scouting Moon Farm, but who else would have taken this route in?

"For now, please focus on getting us inside, Spencer," Yude said, moving his head away from the evidence that someone else had broken in through this very same skylight.

"All right. Sorry," Spencer mumbled. He crouched beside the skylight and for the first time, looked into the building below. What he saw there wasn't anything like what he'd expected.

There were no bears in cages, and thankfully there weren't any *parts* of bears anywhere in sight. Instead, the big, brightly lit room below looked like some kind of heavy-duty gym. It reminded him of the Bear Guard's training field and the Bear Stealth practice course that was in Bearhaven's schoolyard.

Obstacles were placed around the cement floor. A cluster of stone pillars ran from the floor to the ceiling in one section of the room. They looked like they were supposed to simulate trees, and Spencer got a terrible feeling that training to get through them might prepare someone to get through Bearhaven's outer tree wall. He continued to search the room. Near the cement columns, Spencer spotted an enormous, perfectly round boulder. It looked like it had been abandoned mid roll. Spencer spotted a stack of monster-truck-sized tires and various other heavy-looking objects strewn about, but the room was so big he couldn't see all of it through the skylight.

"Yude," Spencer whispered. "What is this place?"

"It's a training room," Yude answered.

"A training room for what?" Spencer didn't remember any mention of training in B.D.'s explanation of bear smuggling.

"Bears, I would assume."

"But—" Before Spencer could ask *why* bears were being trained at Moon Farm, Yude cut him off.

"Operative, now is not the time for questions. The bears are held on the first and second floors. We have to get in to find Kate, and you're the only thing stopping us from doing that. Now open the window."

Spencer snapped his attention back to the crowbar. Yude was right, there wasn't time to waste on questions, but Spencer had a feeling the real reason Yude wouldn't answer was that he didn't know why bears would be trained here, either. Spencer fit the tip of the crowbar into the seam between the glass and its frame and slowly levered the skylight open. He was careful not to make a single sound. After a moment, the job was done. Eager to see what else the mysterious training room held, he poked his head through the skylight.

If Spencer's hands hadn't been gripping the edges of the window frame, keeping him from falling from the roof to the cement floor, he'd have clapped a hand over his mouth to keep himself from screaming. Instead, it took everything in him to keep even the tiniest gasp from escaping his lips. His heart started hammering in his chest. As quickly as he could, he pulled his head out of the building and scrambled back a few feet.

"Margo!" he whispered. "And Ivan! They're in there!"

"Did they see you?" Yude asked urgently.

"No," Spencer whispered. "They have their backs turned."

Margo's raspy voice drifted up through the skylight, but she was too far away. Spencer couldn't make out her words.

"What's she saying?" Yude asked. "Humans who aren't wearing Ear-COMs don't translate."

"I don't know," Spencer whispered. "I can't hear her well enough." Spencer crept closer to the edge of the skylight so he could get a view of the room below. He strained to hear more, but Margo was moving toward the far side of the room as she spoke to Ivan.

"What could the Lalickis being here mean?" he whispered urgently to Yude and Aldo. "Do you think Uncle Mark is here? And Mom and Dad?!"

"Or did they kidnap Kate?!" Aldo whispered. "They must have been the two unidentified humans outside Bearhaven."

"No, that can't be right," Spencer answered before Yude could. "They were in the picture that Uncle Mark got. They were part of his lead. Mom and Dad must—"

"Quiet," Yude growled. His eyes flashed angrily from Spencer to Aldo. "There are only three of us on this mission now. Kate's chances of getting out of here are already in jeopardy. If you two can't *focus*, she may never see Bearhaven again. Do you understand me?" Yude's fangs flashed in the moonlight. His tone was biting. "We aren't solving a mystery tonight, we're saving a cub's life. Now pull it together."

Out of the corner of his eye, Spencer saw Aldo drop his head.

"Sorry, Yude," the younger bear mumbled.

Spencer whispered an apology of his own.

Yude padded closer to the skylight and lowered his head to the opening. "We have to go through that room," he said after a moment. "There's no other way to gain access. There are no doors that join the two halves of the building from the inside. The illegal staff uses a separate dock and there's a much more heavily guarded entrance. We have to get through here."

"What about Margo and Ivan?" Aldo piped up.

"We'll have to get them out of the room."

"How are we supposed to do that?" Spencer whispered, as much to himself as to Aldo and Yude.

Both bears turned to look at him at the same time. Spencer gulped.

"Me?" he managed to say.

"You have the best chance of getting into the room unnoticed," Yude said. "And you're the only one who can understand what they're saying once you're in. How's your Bear Stealth?"

"I've trained," Spencer answered. He didn't feel as confident as he sounded. He searched Yude's face. Could he really trust the bear? Or was Yude just going to use Spencer for bait? Yude looked back. The anger Spencer had grown used to seeing in the bear's eyes was completely gone. "I can do it," he said at last.

"Good," Yude said. "We'll lower you down."

29

Spencer was suspended in the open skylight. His whole body was shaking. One wrong move and he'd plummet to the cement floor and into the clutches of Margo and Ivan Lalicki. The back of Spencer's shirt was clamped between Aldo's teeth. The bear was waiting for the signal to lower Spencer into the room, and Spencer was waiting for Margo and Ivan to make some sound that would cover the thud of his feet hitting the floor when Aldo let him go. Spencer could feel his shirt starting to slip from between the bear's clamped jaws.

In the room below, Margo and Ivan stood with their backs turned, their attention absorbed by a single bear in a cage. Margo had a clipboard in one hand and a remote control in the other. *They're testing the bear,* Spencer thought. He knew enough about Margo's remote control to know that the bear in the cage was microchipped, and Margo had complete control over its actions by using the remote control. Suddenly, Margo erupted into loud hacking coughs.

Finally! Spencer pointed down, and Aldo lowered him as far as he could, then opened his mouth and let Spencer go. Spencer's feet hit the floor just as Margo stopped coughing. Spencer caught his breath and ducked behind a nearby boulder. He looked up at the open skylight; Yude and Aldo were both watching him. At least if anything went wrong, there were two bears who could come to his rescue.

Reassured, Spencer moved to peek around the boulder. Before he could see anything, Margo's voice sent him back into hiding.

"I'm going to run him through it one more time and then we're leaving. Are you listening to me, Ivan? Put that boulder down," she commanded.

Bang! What Spencer guessed was the sound of the boulder hitting the cement floor made him jump.

"They're leaving soon," Spencer whispered so quietly he wasn't sure the Ear-COM would pick up his message to Yude and Aldo. He wanted to feel relieved. He wouldn't have to trick the Lalickis into leaving the training room long enough for Bearhaven's team to get into the building, but he didn't know what Margo meant when she said she was going to "run him through it one more time."

Whoosh! An enormous bear ran right past the boulder at full speed.

Spencer clapped a hand over his mouth to stop himself from screaming. The bear had come within a few feet of Spencer's hiding spot, and now he was weaving through the cement pillars. Margo was running the bear through the training course! Spencer looked to the skylight; Yude and Aldo watched the bear intently. Aldo looked ready to launch himself into the room, and Yude's expression was grim.

Spencer was trapped. When the bear turned to go back to Margo, he would find Spencer, but if Spencer moved now, Margo and Ivan would catch him. Adrenaline pounded through Spencer's veins as he watched the bear race through the obstacle course of cement pillars. His paws hit the ground heavily with every stride. He was implanted with a microchip. There was no doubt about that. The bear's motions were more robotic than the way Bearhaven's bears moved. His paws landed too heavily on the floor, as though he didn't have any real control over where they took him next.

"That's it," Margo said. Spencer held his breath. "He's focused now. He'll perform well tonight."

Spencer kept his eyes glued to the microchipped bear, who abruptly stopped weaving through the tightly packed pillars. The bear turned and broke into a run. His eyes locked on Spencer. His nose and ears twitched. He was heading straight for the boulder, straight for Spencer. Spencer froze. He wanted to scream and scramble away, but he couldn't get himself to move.

"We're here, Spencer," Yude said into the Ear-COM urgently. "We're coming in five . . . four . . ." Spencer looked up. Yude's eyes were locked on the bear. It looked like he and Aldo were going to drop into the room the second the bear got too close. Spencer tore his eyes away, returning his attention to the microchipped bear racing straight—no, the bear wasn't racing straight at him.

"Three . . . two . . ." Yude counted.

"Wait!" Spencer hissed.

The microchipped bear was running at full speed back the way he'd come. He was only a few paces away now, and though his eyes were on Spencer, his feet continued to pound in the direction of Margo and Ivan. *The microchip won't let him change his course!* Spencer realized.

"Spencer?" Yude asked, his voice tense.

"He's going to miss me," Spencer whispered, hoping as hard as he could that he was right. He was. The bear ran past at full speed. He came within a few feet of Spencer, who crouched pressed up against the boulder, but never stopped running in a straight line, retracing his steps to Margo, and to his cage.

A moment later, Spencer heard the clanking sound of a cage door being closed.

"We're done here, Ivan. Put a chain on him and let's go," Margo barked. "The boss and his *special companion* don't like to wait." She spat out the words "special companion" like they tasted bad, but that wasn't what worried Spencer. What worried him was that Margo's boss was waiting for her.

Margo's boss was Pam.

Spencer listened carefully to the sound of the cage door being opened and the clanking of chains.

"Hurry up, Ivan," Margo groaned. A few seconds later, Spencer heard the Lalickis open a door and the sound of a chain clattering out of the room. The door slammed shut.

Spencer took a deep breath and peered around the side of the boulder. On the far side of the room, the bear cage stood empty. The Lalickis and their microchipped bear were gone.

"That bear was microchipped," Spencer reported through his Ear-COM. "Margo was preparing him for some kind of performance for Pam tonight." He looked up into the skylight at Yude and Aldo. "They're gone now. Let's go."

30

Spencer, Aldo, and Yude stood huddled in the dimly lit stairwell. Spencer had one hand wrapped around the jade bear in his pocket, and his lips were sealed shut. Now that he knew Margo and Ivan were here, it was taking all his willpower not to launch into a long string of questions about the possibility of Mom and Dad being somewhere at Moon Farm.

Yude's voice rumbled in Spencer's ear as the bear updated B.D., Evarita, and Professor Weaver on the new developments. Aldo looked as though he was listening to Yude intently, obviously eager to continue the hunt for Kate, and Spencer tuned out the messages coming through his Ear-COM. He already knew what Yude was communicating to the others. Instead, he silently reviewed the information they'd gathered on the mission so far. He wanted it to be a coincidence that Margo and Ivan were here training a microchipped bear—in the same place Kate was taken after her kidnapping. But he knew all the pieces must somehow be connected and that Pam, Mom, and Dad fit into the puzzle somehow, too. Spencer tried to make sense of everything, but, before he could, his thoughts were abruptly interrupted.

"Disconnect," Yude said. "Aldo, Spencer." The bear reconnected their Ear-COMs immediately. "With Margo and Ivan here, Moon Farm is more dangerous than we expected. We need to locate Kate quickly, and we need to start—" Yude suddenly stopped talking. His ears twitched back and forth.

"What's—" Spencer started, but Yude cut him off.

"Quiet." The bear stood alert. "Do you hear that?"

Spencer held his breath, listening.

Thump. Thump. Thump. Thump.

Yes, he heard it, too. It sounded like a drum beating.

"It's coming from outside." Aldo rushed down a few stairs to a window. Spencer and Yude followed, crowding in around Aldo to get a view of the courtyard behind the building. Spencer tried to stifle a gasp.

The courtyard on the back side of the building was surrounded by towering cement walls. It looked like a big stone cell, and it was filled with bears.

Thump. Thump. Thump. Thump.

There wasn't a drum anywhere in sight. The sound was coming from the bears. They were lined up in perfect, even rows, and they were marching in unison back and forth. When the first bear in each column reached the cement wall to the left, a whistle blew, and they all stopped. A whistle blew again, they all turned. When the whistle blew a third time, the columns of bears marched until they reached the cement wall to the right. It looked like a drill, as if the bears were soldiers preparing to march into battle.

"How many are there?" Spencer whispered once they'd witnessed the bears make a few passes across the courtyard.

"I count eighty-eight. Eleven rows. Eight bears in each row. But Kate is not among them," Yude answered.

Eighty-eight? The number sounded weirdly familiar, but Spencer didn't know why. His eyes flew down the columns of bears. Was Yude sure Kate wasn't one of them? No. All these bears were way too big to be a cub. He squinted. The bears' movements were stiff, robotic.

"They're microchipped," he whispered. "All of them." What could Margo and Pam possibly need eighty-eight microchipped bears for? His stomach flopped. Whatever it was, it wasn't good.

Spencer tore his eyes away from the rows of marching bears. He searched the far side of the courtyard. He spotted Margo first. She was standing on a small platform with a whistle between her lips and a remote control clutched in her hands. She had a satisfied sneer on her face as she watched the bears march according to her commands. This was the performance she'd been preparing the bear in the training room for.

To one side of the platform, next to Margo as always, Spencer spotted Ivan, and behind him, a huge screen that covered the stone wall. Pam's live image sat in the center of the video screen, surveying the courtyard below. He wore a satisfied expression on his face as he watched the bears marching back and forth in front of him. His throne framed him creepily. The row of bear teeth spiking the top of the throne gleamed like they'd just been polished. Each of the armrests ended in a hollowed-out bear paw, complete with space for Pam to slide his long, clawlike nails in where the bear's claws would have been.

Now that Spencer had been told what bear-part trading was, he was sure everything Pam's throne was made of had come from real bears. He shuddered. And, if the throne itself wasn't bad enough, then there was Pam. The potbellied man sat perched on fur cushions. His glossy black hair was smoothed perfectly into place. He looked amused as the bears marched back and forth in front of him. He looked evil.

"I've seen enough," Yude said. "We'll tell the council everything when we return to Bearhaven. Come on."

Yude and Aldo started to back away.

"Wait!" Spencer whispered. He kept staring at the screen. The last time he'd seen Mom she'd been with Pam, dressed as his maid. There was someone in the shadows behind Pam's throne. *Is it Mom?* He wanted it to be her and didn't want it to be her at the same time. He was desperate to see her again, but if she wasn't there, maybe that meant Uncle Mark had rescued her and Dad already. His mind was racing.

"Spencer." Yude's voice was firm. "We're moving *now*."

Just then, Pam lifted a clawed hand. Yude and Aldo stopped. Pam waved to whoever was standing in the shadows behind his throne to come forward. A second later, a huge, jet-black bear stepped into the light beside Pam. There was a gold, jeweled collar around the bear's neck and a furless patch of skin at its jaw.

"His special companion," Spencer whispered.

"Who is she?" Aldo asked.

"I don't know," Yude answered.

The huge bear sat back on her haunches. She surveyed the scene in the courtyard, her expression stony. Whoever she was, that bear was important to Pam. Spencer searched the shadows on the screen again, holding on to his hope that Mom might be there. She wasn't. Spencer stepped away from the window. He didn't know what Mom's absence meant or where she might be, but he didn't need to see any more of Pam, his bear companion, or the microchipped army in the courtyard below.

31

"The cage rooms are this way," Yude said, starting down the stairs to the second floor. "Aldo, you'll start by smelling for Kate at the entrance to each room. You should be close enough then to pick up her scent."

"No." Aldo's voice was firm. His snout was twitching rapidly back and forth and he'd risen onto his hind legs.

"Excuse me?" Yude asked, turning back.

"I mean she's not down there." Aldo said. He slowly turned his back on Spencer and Yude. He took a step back up the stairwell, then paused, turning his head from side to side as he sniffed. All of a sudden, Aldo launched himself up the stairs, racing toward the third floor. Yude lumbered up the steps, trying to catch up to the younger bear. Spencer followed as quickly as he could. Aldo stopped at the closed door to the third floor training room. To one side of the door, a spiral staircase Spencer hadn't noticed before led upward. *The stairs to the tower!*

"She's up there," Aldo growled. "I can smell her."

"You're sure?" Yude asked, his voice tense for the first time all night.

"What's wrong?" Aldo turned back to Yude.

"If you're sure Kate's in this tower, then we got here just in time," Yude answered. "There's a helicopter pad on the tower roof, and all Moon Farm shipments—the illegal ones—leave by helicopter. If Kate's in there, she's already been sold. She must be scheduled to ship in the morning."

Spencer reached into his pocket for the jade bear. "Sold?" he asked quietly. "You mean—"

"I mean that if Kate doesn't leave Moon Farm with us tonight, she'll leave on a helicopter tomorrow morning. There's no telling where she'll go or what shape she'll be in, and we'll probably never find out."

Aldo growled and shook his head. "We have to get her out of there." He put a claw on the first stair up into the tower, waiting for Yude to give him the signal to go.

"Spencer, check that everyone's still assembled in the courtyard," Yude ordered. "Aldo, stand guard while I update B.D. Disconnect."

Spencer raced to the closest window. The scene in the courtyard looked the same. The harsh yellow beams of a few spotlights illuminated everything. The bears were still in formation, Margo was still poised on her platform, ready to issue the next command, and Pam and his enormous bear companion were still projected on their screen. Now, though, Pam was speaking. His voice was high-pitched and sickly sweet, just like Spencer remembered it.

"The cub you brought in was a promising catch, Margo," Pam screeched from his spot in the middle of the video screen. "We're closing in on them. Continue the preparations. When we find Bearhaven, we'll be ready. Now," Pam went on theatrically. "On to the next order of business."

Spencer didn't stay to find out what the next order of business was. What he'd heard was bad enough. It *was* Margo and Ivan who'd kidnapped Kate after all—and Pam, and his army of microchipped bears, were coming for Bearhaven. He rushed back to rejoin the team.

"Yude, Aldo," he said, reconnecting their Ear-COMs. "They're still assembled down there." Spencer stopped himself from adding the details of what Pam had said. By now he'd learned that distracting from this mission's goal—saving Kate—wasn't what a trained operative was supposed to do. Bearhaven would have time to stop Pam later. It had to. But Kate only had until morning.

"All right, here's how we're going to proceed." Yude launched into plans for the next step in the mission. "You two are going into the tower. Aldo, Kate will respond best to seeing you. Spencer, Aldo needs a human operative with him. I'm going back to the roof. I can stand guard there while I keep an eye on the courtyard and plan our evacuation with the rest of the team. We'll need the others ready for the exit as soon as you have Kate.

"There are two ways into the tower," Yude continued. "This stairwell and a ladder on the outside of the tower. Take the stairs now. But bring her down the ladder and meet me on the roof. It's the fastest way out. We'll leave from there as quickly as we can."

"See you on the roof," Aldo said, nodding to Yude. "Let's go get Kate," he added to Spencer, then turned and started up the stairs.

Before Spencer could reply to Yude himself, Aldo had disappeared around the first turn in the spiral staircase that led up into the tower. Spencer was afraid to lose Aldo in the dark. He raced up the windowless staircase after the bear, but it was no use. Aldo's shadow sped farther and farther into the dark ahead, until Spencer could only barely hear the distant sound of claws hitting stone steps.

"Spencer, are you back there?" Aldo said into Spencer's Ear-COM after a few moments had passed.

"I'm coming as fast as I can!" Spencer answered, already out of breath. "Aren't you supposed to be protecting me anyway?" he added in a mumble, a little bothered by being left behind. He continued up the stairs. It was impossible for him to see anything farther than a few feet ahead of him. He squinted, searching the stone walls on either side of him as he climbed, but he hadn't passed a single door yet. A moment later an enormous dark shadow rushed toward him.

"Ahhh!" Spencer yelled, then clapped a hand over his mouth, but it was too late. His scream echoed through the tower.

"What's going on?!" Yude practically bellowed through the Ear-COMs.

"It's me!" Aldo hissed. "I was just coming back for Spencer. Hurry, Spencer, climb on."

"Sorry," Spencer muttered. He wanted to be angry at Aldo for descending out of the dark with no warning, but he was too relieved to be reunited with the bear. He reached for the dark outline that he knew was Aldo and took two fistfuls of the bear's fur. Spencer swung onto Aldo's back. "Let's go."

Aldo lurched forward, and in what seemed like seconds, they'd reached the top of the winding staircase. Aldo leaped off the last step and slid to a stop. Spencer jumped off the bear's back. An open door to the rooftop helicopter pad allowed the moon to light the small landing where he and Aldo now stood. Across from the door to the roof, there was a closed metal door. Aldo moved to crouch in front of it on all fours. He lowered his snout to sniff at the sliver of space between the door and the floor.

"She's here," he growled.

Spencer squeezed in beside the bear. He grabbed the doorknob and tried to turn it. Only when it didn't turn did Spencer take a good look at the electric keypad above the doorknob.

Screech! Spencer flinched at the sound of Aldo's claws scraping against metal.

Aldo's muscles were straining as he attempted to pry the locked door off its hinges. His claws were hooked in the inch of space between the door and the floor. The door didn't budge. The electronic lock sealed it shut. Spencer reached forward and pressed a few random numbers on the keypad. After he'd put in four digits, a red light flashed.

It's a four number code. Now he knew that much.

Spencer was going to have to come up with the right four numbers in the right order before anyone discovered them. There was no other way in, but where was he supposed to start?

Aldo grunted and strained against the door. Spencer reached into his pocket and pulled out the jade bear. He needed a second to think. Kate was probably only a few feet away. Getting to her was up to him.

He examined the familiar stone figurine in his palm. The jade bear was standing on its hind legs the way real bears did in order to see, hear, and smell better. Mom and Dad said bears weren't trying to be aggressive when they rose into that position. They were trying to learn about their surroundings so they could protect themselves if they needed to. Spencer let his hand hover over the keypad, his mind starting to race. He knew a lot about bears. Mom and Dad loved to tell him facts about the eight different bear species, and plenty of those facts had numbers in them. Pam was clearly obsessed with bears. Maybe bears were the very key Spencer needed.

A brown bear has five claws on each of its four feet. 5-5-5-5, he typed. A red light flashed.

Male polar bears weigh up to seventeen hundred pounds. 1-7-0-0. The red light flashed again.

There had to be something more specific. Why hadn't he counted the teeth that lined the top of Pam's throne? Or the number of shelves in each tower in the warehouse? *Anything* that might help him now.

Frustrated, Spencer shoved his jade bear back into his pocket. Who was he kidding? A bunch of random numbers about bears was not going to open this door. He was just a novice, and between this electronic lock and the bear army in the back courtyard, Moon Farm was a fortress.

Wait! The marching bears! Yude had said there were eighty-eight of them. Suddenly, Spencer realized why eighty-eight had sounded so familiar when Yude said it. Eighty-eight was right in the middle of the license plate number that led them to Moon Farm! Spencer had read it out to Evarita himself. "M-0-8-8-0-N-F." The number eighty-eight obviously meant something to Pam!

0-8-8-0, he keyed. The light flashed green.

Yes! Without sparing a second, he swung the metal door open. Aldo nearly knocked Spencer over as he barreled into the dimly lit room. Spencer ran in after the bear. He skidded to a stop the moment he was inside.

"Kate!" he cried.

A metal collar was fastened around Kate's neck. A ring at the back of the collar was attached to a thick chain that was bolted into the cement wall. Kate struggled to lift her head from the floor. Her shackles were too heavy. She lay slumped on the cement, a prisoner beside the wooden crate she was meant to be shipped out in.

32

Spencer didn't want to look around the room. It was *way* too scary, but he had to find the key to the collar around Kate's neck.

"Is it definitely in here?" he asked Yude over the Ear-COM one more time.

"Yes." Yude was certain. The key to unlocking Kate was in the shipping room. "You have to find it," he ordered. Spencer looked up at Aldo. The bear was clawing at Kate's chain where it was bolted into the stone wall. He growled angrily. Spencer could tell Aldo's desperation was mounting. Spencer felt the same way. The sight of Kate like this was horrible.

Spencer was crouching beside the cub. She was still curled in a ball on the cement floor. His hand was on her paw, but she hadn't looked at him yet. She whimpered every so often but hadn't managed to raise her head. The chain and collar were too heavy.

"Yude," Spencer said quietly. "Do you have any ginger root?"

"Yes. Are you hurt?" The bear's answer was calm but came quickly.

"Not me. They put a tag through Kate's ear. It doesn't look good." Spencer's stomach lurched when he looked down at Kate's swollen ear. Her chestnut-colored fur was matted with blood where a gold metal tag in the shape of a bear was pierced through. The numbers 5758 were engraved on the metal tag.

"Just focus on getting her out of there, Spencer. Start with finding the key."

Spencer didn't want to leave Kate's side, but Yude was right. If they didn't get her out of Moon Farm, the infection caused by the tag in her ear would be the least of Kate's problems.

"Aldo," Spencer called to the bear. "Can you come be with Kate? I have to look for the key, and . . . I don't think that's going to work." Spencer nodded to the barely visible scratches Aldo's claws had made in the stone wall around Kate's chain.

The bear gave a frustrated snarl and slumped down to all fours. He quickly padded over to Kate's side.

Spencer patted the cub's paw once more in a gesture he hoped felt reassuring, then stood up. He took in the room around them. It was round, just like the tower, and had four barred windows. The crate next to Kate was made of wood, with three small air holes drilled into each side. On the wall behind the crate there was a huge digital display listing sale details. Spencer scanned the list. Each entry on the list was more horrible than the last.

5756—circus—shipped.
5757—thirty-two teeth—shipped.
5757—hide—shipped.

5757—four paws—shipped.

The next number on the board matched the number on the tag in Kate's ear.

5758—private collector—awaiting shipment.

Spencer wanted to smash the board with the hammer in his mission pack. He wanted to find a way to put a stop to Moon Farm's operations tonight so no bear would ever have to be shipped out of this room again. Kate whimpered, snapping Spencer's attention back to the task at hand: finding the key to Kate's collar.

On the far side of the room there was a big, sleek black desk. Its surface was threateningly empty, like a table in a lab, or a hospital. There were only two things on the desk: a big black computer, its screen dark, and a gold paperweight in the shape of a bear's head, its jaws open in a roar. Spencer ran over to the desk. He did a lap around it, searching for a drawer where the key might be hidden. There wasn't one. He ran his hands along the underside of the desk thinking maybe the key was attached there. It wasn't.

"It has to be here *somewhere*," he said, talking to himself. His eyes landing on the gold paperweight.

"It's there." Yude's voice surprised Spencer. He'd forgotten the Ear-COM would transmit his words into Yude and Aldo's ears, even when Spencer was only thinking aloud.

Spencer reached for the large gold paperweight with both hands.

"Ugh!" he grunted. The bear head paperweight was too heavy to lift, so he stepped closer. The space between the open golden jaws looked like a dark cavern with two rows of gleaming fangs at the opening. Before he could talk himself out of it, he darted his hand into the bear's mouth. He felt something right away. Spencer grabbed it and pulled his hand out. It was a key.

"I have it!" he shouted, and sprinted to Kate's side.

"Hurry!" Aldo urged, making space for Spencer beside the cub. Spencer knelt down and reached for the collar. Kate shrank away.

"It's okay, Kate," Spencer whispered. "We're getting you out of here." He knew she wouldn't be able to understand him without her BEAR-COM, but he hoped the tone of his voice might still reassure her. He reached for the collar again. This time, Kate let him take hold of it. He fit the key into the collar's lock and turned it. The collar and chain clattered to the floor.

Aldo moved forward, gently nudging Kate to all fours. Without the metal around her neck, she managed to stand, but her legs shook, as though she was only barely strong enough to stay upright. Aldo stepped even closer. Kate leaned against him for support.

"Okay, we have her," Spencer reported. "But she's not doing so well."

Yude didn't answer.

"Yude?"

Still nothing.

"Yude," Aldo tried.

Spencer, Aldo, and the barely standing Kate waited, frozen in the silent shipping room for Yude's answer. It didn't come.

33

Spencer didn't know where Yude was or what the bear was doing, but there wasn't time to waste. They had to get out of the shipping room and off this island, with or without Yude's instructions.

"Let's move," Aldo said, as though reading Spencer's mind. The bear's voice was confident, but he didn't move an inch. Kate looked like she might collapse if he did.

"How are we going to get her down the ladder?" Spencer looked from Kate to Aldo. "There's no way she can climb on her own."

"I could carry her down, but I don't think she's strong enough to hold on to me," Aldo said. "We're going to have to come up with something,"

"All right, let's think like operatives," Spencer muttered. He quickly ran through each category of his STORM training in his head, searching for a skill that might help them. None of it seemed right. If only he had a specialty talent like Yude with his strategy and Evarita with her background checks. Then Spencer had it. He *did* have a special skill! Knot tying!

Spencer swung his mission pack off his back. Dad had taught Spencer how to tie sailing knots, and Spencer's knot tying had helped him on the mission to save Ro Ro and her cubs. Maybe Dad had been preparing Spencer for Bearhaven missions all along! He pulled a bundle of rope out of the backpack. Kate might not be able to hold on to Aldo for the climb down to the roof below, but maybe Spencer could make it so she didn't have to. A plan was starting to take shape in his mind. He began tying knots in the middle of the length of rope.

"You have an idea?" Aldo asked, eyeing Spencer's knots with concern.

"I'm going to make a harness and tie her to you." Spencer's fingers flew across the rope as he fashioned a seat of interlocking knots for Kate. He tied the harness around her, careful not to catch her fur in the knots. She kept her head bowed. Then Spencer wound the rope around Aldo, who stood perfectly still, quiet Ragayo rumbling out of his throat.

He must be comforting Kate with those growls, Spencer thought. Whatever the bear was saying, he was saying it so softly that the Ear-COMs weren't even picking it up to translate. Spencer secured as many knots as he could with the length of rope. By the time he stepped back, it looked like Kate was sitting in a hammock or a baby carrier that had been strapped tightly onto the larger bear's back. The cub looked at him for the first time since they'd found her.

Spencer swallowed hard. *"Shala,"* he growled softly, using the Ragayo word for "safe" she'd taught him herself. The knots would hold. They had to.

"Aldo, Spencer." Yude's voice came through Spencer's Ear-COM, startling him.

Where have you been?! Spencer wanted to shout at the bear who was supposed to be leading them. Yude rushed on. "Someone's trying to transmit a large amount of data on the island. It's interfering with the Ear-COM technology. What's your—" Yude's voice cut out again. In the very same moment, a spotlight clicked on above Spencer's head. It shone directly on the section of cement floor where Kate's empty collar and chain now lay. Little red lights popped on, one after another after another all around the room.

"What the . . ." Spencer lifted an arm above his head to shield his eyes.

Aldo bared his teeth and crouched down low. Kate buried her face in her brother's fur.

"What's going on?" Spencer cried.

A roar erupted outside; Spencer ran to one of the barred windows. He could still make out Pam's enormous video screen in the brightly lit courtyard far below, but the image it displayed had changed. Now the screen was split between two separate video feeds. Pam and his huge bear companion were on one half of the screen, and on the other half Spencer saw himself. And Aldo. And Kate.

Spencer spun around. Each of the little red lights that surrounded the room was a camera! The cameras were feeding footage directly into the midnight assembly in the courtyard! Spencer gulped. Pam, Margo, Ivan, and their entire bear army were watching Spencer, Aldo, and Kate's every move.

That roar was the sound of eighty-eight bears growling at once.

"Aldo," Spencer whispered. "Run."

34

The spotlight above Spencer's head suddenly blinked off. He turned back to the barred window and looked out. *No!* The army of bears in the courtyard was storming the building, disappearing into an entrance to the tower below where Spencer, Aldo, and Kate were now.

"They're coming!" Spencer shouted.

"The door!" Aldo yelled at the same time. "Hurry!"

Spencer spun around. The open metal door they'd broken through to get to Kate was swinging shut—fast. The electric keypad was only on the outside of the door. If it shut, they'd be trapped!

Aldo, with Kate tied to his back, raced toward the heavy metal door. It was inches from sealing shut. Spencer broke into a sprint. *We'll never make it!*

BANG!

Spencer opened his mouth to scream but the sound stuck in his throat. Aldo skidded to a stop. The bear crouched low, baring his teeth and snarling at the door.

Spencer's heart thundered in his chest. The door hadn't slammed shut like he'd expected. Instead, at the very last moment, someone had jammed a crowbar into the closing space between the door and the doorframe. Now, whoever was on the other side of the metal door was levering it open. Spencer didn't know whether to help open the door or prepare for an attack from whoever was on the other side.

He heard a grunt, then the sound of metal scraping against metal. The door swung open again. Aldo stepped back a few paces and rose up onto his hind legs, shielding Kate. Spencer kept his eyes on the doorway. A dark figure stood there. The moonlight from the roof outlined a man's body. Spencer could make out the shape of the crowbar gripped in the man's hand. He wielded it like a weapon.

"We're trapped," Spencer whispered, willing the Ear-COM to transmit the message to Yude—wherever he was.

"No, we're not," Aldo said, nodding toward the figure. He dropped back to all fours and broke into a run as Spencer watched in shock.

"Hurry, Spence. You have to get out of here," the man said urgently. "Now, kid!" he yelled as he stepped aside to let Aldo run through the door.

"Uncle Mark?!" Spencer rushed forward.

"Come on!" Uncle Mark turned and ran after Aldo. Spencer followed, his eyes glued to his uncle. It was really him, but *how*?

"How did you know where to find us?!" Spencer called. "Where are Mom and Dad?!"

"No time for questions. We have to get out of here!" Uncle Mark called back.

Spencer ran out onto the roof of the tower after his uncle. Aldo and Kate were already there. The neon outlines of a helicopter pad glowed eerily in the dark. The building was shaking beneath them. The sound of eighty-eight bears thundering up the spiral staircase echoed out of the building.

Uncle Mark spun around. "Give me your mission pack," he demanded. Spencer handed it over as quickly as he could. Uncle Mark grabbed something from his back pocket and shoved it into Spencer's pack before handing the bag back.

"Everything you want to know is in there, Spence—I've got a lead on your parents. You have to trust me, just like I'm trusting you. Take Kate away from this place. I'll meet you back in Bearhaven, I promise." He pulled Spencer into a quick hug. "I'm going to work on holding them off. Get Kate home, operative."

"Wait!" Spencer cried, but it was no use. Uncle Mark was already disappearing back into the dark tower. Spencer resisted the urge to chase his uncle down and demand an explanation. Uncle Mark had called Spencer "operative" because, tonight, that's what Spencer was. There was no time to get distracted by all the unanswered questions filling his head. Growls thundered from the tower. This may be the only chance he, Kate, and Aldo had to get out of here tonight.

"Spencer!" Aldo called from the edge of the roof.

Spencer rushed over. Beside Aldo, the top of a ladder was poking up into the night sky. Spencer looked down and winced. The metal ladder was bolted into the tower's stone wall. It ran from the helicopter pad, where they stood now, down to the roof below, where Yude was supposed to be waiting with a plan for their escape. The ladder was so long that it disappeared into the dark. Spencer couldn't see the end of it, but he knew it was way too far down.

"Spencer, Aldo." It was Yude! Two days ago, Spencer never thought he'd be happy to hear Yude's voice in his ear. Now he was so relieved to be back in communication with the bear he wanted to cheer.

"We're coming down now," Aldo said, mounting the ladder.

"Come as quickly as you can, Pam's army—"

"Is after us. We know." Spencer finished Yude's sentence. The bear didn't answer.

Once Aldo, with Kate tied firmly to his back, had started to descend, Spencer took a deep breath and climbed onto the ladder. Focusing on one rung at a time, Spencer moved down the side of the tower as quickly as he could. Below him, Aldo dropped to the roof, landing on all fours. Spencer was relieved to see that Kate was still securely tied to her brother's back. His knots hadn't slipped an inch.

Spencer made it to the last rung of the ladder and onto the rooftop at the base of the stone tower just as the first of Pam's bears appeared on the helicopter pad.

"Yude," Spencer called.

"I'm here," Yude answered. He stepped out of the tower's pitch-black shadow. "What's the rope for?" he asked immediately.

"We weren't sure Kate could hold on by herself," Aldo answered quickly. The microchipped bears stared down at them, snarling and snapping their jaws on the tower's roof, and a few of them climbed onto the ladder, getting ready to come down.

Yude nodded. "This way." He took off at a gallop, stopping only when he'd reached the edge of the roof. He looked out over the iron railing. Aldo followed, then stopped beside Yude. Spencer sprinted to catch up, but he stopped running a few feet farther from the edge of the roof than Yude and Aldo. Railing or no railing, there was a three-story drop from the roof to the ground below. Just because Spencer understood where his fear of falling came from now didn't mean he'd overcome that fear yet. And their new position on the edge of the roof was giving him a very bad feeling about Yude's escape plan. Yude turned around. He looked over the knotted harness Spencer had made. "Nicely done, Spencer," he said quickly. "Now untie Kate from Aldo, but leave that harness on her and tighten the knots."

Spencer went to work, following Yude's orders. Untying the knots gave him a reason not to look back at the tower. He didn't want to know how close Pam's bears had gotten. Hearing their growls as they approached was bad enough.

Once he'd untied Kate from Aldo then tightened each of the knots in Kate's makeshift harness, Spencer looked back to Yude. The bear was scanning the night sky, searching for something.

"How are we getting off the roof, Yude?" Spencer asked. He couldn't see anything that looked like an escape route, and they'd never have time now to go back through the warehouse. Spencer's heart started to pound. What were they going to do?

Yude started to murmur in Ragayo to Kate. The cub was still shaking, her fur rippling in the moonlight. The Ear-COM didn't translate Yude's unusually soft words, but Spencer heard *shala* for "safe" and *val* for "home" rumble gently out of the older bear's throat.

Spencer couldn't help himself; he looked up at the tower. The first of Pam's bears were already halfway down the ladder. The column of bears descending the rungs above them seemed endless. They were pouring down the tower wall toward Bearhaven's team.

"Yude!" Spencer shouted now. "What are we waiting for?!"

Pow! A flare shot up over the water. Spencer whipped around to see where it had come from. The flare illuminated the ocean beneath it. In the center of its circle of light idled a white speedboat.

"That," Yude answered. "*That's* what we were waiting for."

35

The escape route Yude, B.D., Evarita, and Professor Weaver
had put in place was the worst way out of Moon Farm
Spencer could imagine.

"There *has* to be another way!" he protested. "I'd rather
take my chances with *them*!" he shouted, gesturing angrily
in the direction of the chipped bears that would be dropping
from the tower ladder to the roof any minute.

"You don't have that option," Yude answered. He tested
the steel wire that ran from the iron railing on Moon Farm's
rooftop, over the stone wall surrounding the island, out past
the rocky cliffs, to Bearhaven's boat in the moonlit ocean.
"We installed the zip line while you and Aldo were freeing
Kate. It's secure—Professor Weaver has specially engineered
it to hold up to five hundred pounds."

Still, Spencer didn't trust an exit plan that required him
to jump off a roof. He opened his mouth to refuse one more
time, but Yude cut him off.

"Operative, it's my job to make the plan; it's your job to
follow it. There are eighty-eight bears within two minutes of
overtaking us. This is not a training exercise. This is the only
chance any of us have of ever leaving this island. Now listen

to me. Mission packs are designed to double as harnesses. You have a dozen carabineers in yours for a reason. You're the only one whose hands can clip us to the wire. Now get ready."

There was no sense in arguing. Yude was right, and even if he was wrong, he wasn't giving Spencer any other option. Spencer sprang into action. He dug all the carabineers he had out of his mission pack.

"Aldo, you're going down first," Yude commanded. "You can't take Kate down yourself. Together you'd be too heavy, and Spencer won't be able to reach back to clip more than one other bear to the line after he's clipped himself and Kate. Now get the extra strap out of your mission pack."

Aldo looked as though he wanted to protest leaving his sister, but there wasn't much he could do except obey Yude, either. He ducked his head toward his fur-camouflaged mission pack and retrieved an extra strap with a clip on either end.

"Spencer, help him attach it, and move quickly, operatives."

Yude had said mission packs were meant to double as harnesses. Spencer understood what he was supposed to do before Yude gave the instruction. He found two empty clips on Aldo's mission pack and connected the extra strap, wrapping it around the bear so that it crossed in front of Aldo's chest.

Aldo gently nuzzled Kate for a moment before he ducked under the railing and perched on the few feet of rooftop that lay on the far side of the railing. Spencer gulped. If Aldo made one wrong step, he'd go over the edge in an instant. On the other side of the railing, there was nothing to stop his fall.

Spencer hurried forward with a carabineer in each hand. It was his job to clip Aldo to the zip line, but what if he made a mistake? What if the carabineer was faulty or the straps of Aldo's mission pack weren't strong enough to hold the bear's weight?! He shook the thoughts out of his head. There was no time for imagining all the things that could go wrong. He used a carabineer to clip each of the straps of Aldo's mission pack to the steel wire of the zip line. He stepped back once they were in place.

Thump! Spencer whipped around. The first of the bears had dropped to the roof and was running toward Bearhaven's team. The bear snarled. His jaw popped and his eyes locked on Spencer.

Thump! Another bear dropped from the ladder.

"Now, Aldo!" he heard Yude command behind him. Spencer turned back just in time to see Aldo push off the roof. Spencer gasped; he wanted to reach out and grab Aldo to stop the bear from plummeting to the ground, but Aldo wasn't falling. The zip line was carrying him, just like Yude had said it would. In the moonlight, Spencer watched as the bear was carried out over the courtyard, then the stone wall, then the cliffs, then the ocean.

Thump! Thump! Spencer didn't have to turn to know that two more bears were on the roof, racing toward him now.

"Hurry, Spencer!" Yude growled. Spencer rushed forward. He ducked under the railing and stepped onto the unguarded sliver of roof on the other side. His hands were filled with carabineers.

"Clip yourself and Kate in now," Yude ordered, guiding Kate with her rope harness under the railing to stand beside

Spencer. "You'll go down together. I'll hold them off." Yude lunged away, his teeth bared. Spencer moved closer to Kate's side. The cub was shaking and whimpering. Her eyes were wide with fear. The sounds of bears locked in battle surrounded them. How long could Yude hold them off?

Spencer hooked Kate's knotted rope harness to the wire with two carabineers. He secured his mission pack on his back and used a carabineer to clip each strap to the steel wire. He tried not to look down or think about what he had to do next.

"Wait!" Spencer stopped himself from going any farther. He and Kate couldn't leave until Yude was clipped to the wire, or Yude would be left with no way to escape the bears that were rapidly descending on them now.

Spencer turned back to the roof. Yude was fighting off three bears. Four more were closing in on them. Yude swiped a claw at one bear and bared his teeth at another. One of the three bears snarled and launched himself at Yude; his claws made contact with Yude's stomach.

"Yude!" Spencer cried. The bears would reach him and Kate any second now. Spencer would have no choice but to go. "Hurry! I have to clip you to the wire!"

Yude turned and ran straight at Spencer and Kate. Pam's bears followed close behind, and another dozen were thundering across the roof now. Spencer had two carabineers ready. The second Yude ducked under the iron railing, Spencer clipped the bear on.

Three bears were suddenly on top of Yude, growling and biting. They reached for Spencer and Kate.

"Go—" Yude's command was cut short as a bear's teeth sank into his back.

Claws swiped at Spencer, and growls and snarls sounded all around him. He wrapped his arms around Kate and leaped off the roof.

36

Kate's chestnut-colored fur kept getting in Spencer's eyes as they careened through the air. He held on to her tighter, terrified the knots of her harness would give way as they flew down the steel wire toward Bearhaven's boat. The straps of his backpack were cutting into his shoulders, but Spencer ignored them. His determination to get Kate to safety pushed every other thought away. The wind whipped past his face, and his arms were burning from holding on to Kate so hard, but the zip line was working. They were going to make it.

They zoomed over the stone wall surrounding Moon Farm, past the rocky cliffs, and over the water, flying lower and lower every second. Spencer craned his neck, trying to see out past Kate's fur. He barely got a glimpse of what was ahead before they hit it a second later.

Spencer and Kate made contact with the deck of Bearhaven's speedboat. An inflated lifeboat softened their landing, but the sudden stop knocked the wind out of Spencer's lungs. Before he could recover, Evarita was above him, unclipping him and Kate from the wire that Spencer could now see wasn't attached to the boat at all. It was anchored in the water behind the boat, secured, Spencer guessed, in the ocean floor.

"You made it!" Evarita cried. She helped him to his feet and tugged him out of the path of the zip line as Professor Weaver, B.D., and Aldo surrounded Kate, helping her carefully to the back of the boat.

Spencer ran to the side of the speedboat and searched the length of the zip line. "Yude was being attacked!" he shouted. "Where is he?" He didn't see the bear on the wire. The roof of Moon Farm was too far away; he couldn't make it out in the dark.

"ARGHH!" Yude's howl of pain filled Spencer's ear.

"They're hurting him!" Spencer cried.

"Team." B.D.'s voice connected their Ear-COMs. "He's on the wire." The Head of the Guard lumbered over to Spencer's side, and together they focused on the zip line. After a second, Yude came into view, flying toward them. Spencer started to relax. They were all going to make it!

Yude cleared Moon Farm's stone wall and sped out past the cliffs. He was halfway across the stretch of ocean that lay between himself and the safety of Bearhaven's speedboat when the zip line suddenly went slack.

"They severed the wire!" B.D. yelled.

Spencer watched in horror as Yude plummeted into the ocean. Evarita sprinted into the cabin. A second later, the speedboat's idling engine roared to life.

"Hold on!" Evarita called. She hit the throttle. The force of the sudden acceleration threw Spencer backward onto the deck. The speedboat skimmed across the water until Evarita cut the engine, turning the boat hard. "I can't get any closer!" she shouted. "I can't see the wire! If it gets caught in the engine, we'll never get away."

Spencer scrambled to his feet. He saw Yude thrashing in the water several yards away. The bear was still clipped to the wire, which was weighing him down. Spencer climbed up on the side of the boat. He'd trained for this.

"I'm going in!" he yelled. Before anyone could stop him, he dove into the cold, dark ocean. He swam as hard as he could toward Yude.

"Spencer, no!" Evarita yelled.

A second later, an enormous jet-black mass hit the water beside Spencer. It was B.D.

"Come on!" the bear shouted. He swam out to Yude, reaching him just after Spencer did. Yude continued to thrash. He was bleeding, and even in the dark, Spencer could see the bear was getting weaker by the second. "Unclip him, Spencer," B.D. ordered. Spencer tread water as he struggled to unhook the two carabineers from the heavy, sinking wire.

"He's free!" he shouted once Yude's mission pack was unclipped from the steel wire. Spencer wrapped his arms around the injured bear, and B.D. clamped his mouth onto the skin at the back of Yude's neck. They started to swim. Together, B.D. and Spencer got Yude to the side of the speedboat. Aldo helped B.D. aboard, then the large bear pulled Yude out behind him. Evarita dragged Spencer out of the water.

"Spencer—" she started in a reprimanding tone, then seemed to decide against scolding him. She hugged him instead. "That was really brave. Now put on a life vest and try to stay *on* the boat until we're back at the dock, okay?"

Spencer pulled his life vest tightly around himself and buckled it. He tried to catch his breath, but before he could, he was gasping at the sight of blinding lights heading straight for them. "Evarita!" he managed to shout, pointing at the lights as they sped closer and closer.

Evarita whipped around. "Team!" she cried. "They're after us! Everyone get down!" She hurtled into the driver's cabin and, with a roar from the engine and a huge lurch that sent Spencer careening back down to the boat deck, hit the throttle. B.D., Professor Weaver, and Aldo scrambled unsteadily to the back of the boat, where they could stand guard over Kate and the wounded Yude.

Spencer crawled across the deck, reaching for the railing on the side of the boat to keep himself from being tossed into the ocean. Bearhaven's speedboat seemed to be flying just above the water, knocking into the waves and bumping back up into the air every few seconds. Spencer craned his neck. The boat behind them was close, too close, and keeping up, despite the fact that it looked rusty and patched together. Spencer could just make out *M.F. Tidal Control* painted in peeling letters on its side. *Uh-oh.* Spencer had one guess as to who was on that boat. As it gained on them, he saw he was right.

Margo was behind the wheel of the *M.F. Tidal Control,* her greenish hair whipping back and forth across her face. Crouched in the bow, with something tucked under one arm like a football, was Ivan.

"They're getting closer!" Spencer shouted.

"Faster, Evarita!" Professor Weaver's voice called through the Ear-COMs.

The *Tidal Control* was so close now, Spencer could see the look of fury on Ivan's face and the look of disgust on Margo's. Spencer's eyes widened as the giant wound up and hurled something at Bearhaven's speedboat.

Ivan hit his mark.

Bam! Something hard hit the deck beside Spencer. He reached for what Ivan had thrown. It was a solid cement teddy bear the size of a grapefruit. *M.F.* was carved into its chest. If it had hit him or anyone else on Bearhaven's team—human or bear—it would have really *really* hurt.

"Spencer!" B.D. shouted.

Bam! Another cement bear hit the speedboat a few inches from where Spencer's hand had just been.

"Faster, Evarita!" Professor Weaver called again. But the speedboat shuddered underneath them. They were going as fast as they could.

37

The speedboat bucked as it flew across the water. Spencer grasped for anything to hold on to as he crawled toward the awning-covered stern. He was afraid he'd be thrown overboard at any moment or knocked unconscious by one of Ivan's stone missiles. The *Tidal Control* was looming right behind them as he took cover under the awning with Bearhaven's bears.

Kate was crouched on the deck of the boat. She was partly shielded by one of the boat's bench seats. Aldo was beside her, and Professor Weaver hovered above, offering as much protection as their bodies could. Kate looked afraid, but her eyes were open, and Spencer didn't think she was shaking anymore. *Being reunited with Professor Weaver and Aldo must already be helping.* Spencer wasn't surprised. No matter where he was, or what was happening around him, when he and Mom and Dad were back together again, he'd feel better, too.

Stretched out on the deck beside Aldo and Kate was Yude. He looked weak and his eyes were closed. He hardly even flinched at the banging sound of Ivan's cement bears hitting the speedboat. B.D. was stationed beside the wounded bear. The Head of the Guard had one paw on a mission pack that was pressed against Yude's chest. Spencer didn't have to ask;

he knew B.D. was applying pressure to try to stop Yude's bleeding.

Spencer squeezed into the little bit of space between Yude and Aldo. He tried not to think about what would happen to Kate and the rest of them if Margo and Ivan caught them now. The list of sales in the Moon Farm shipping room flashed into Spencer's head. Outrunning the *M.F. Tidal Control* was their only hope. He glared back at the boat behind them.

Wait . . . it wasn't as close as it had been a second ago.

"I think we're losing them!" he yelled at the top of his lungs. "They're slowing down!"

Professor Weaver lifted his head, relief flashing across his face. "We haven't lost them yet," he called back, and urged Evarita on.

"They're sinking!" Spencer cried, hardly believing the words as they flew out of his mouth. The *Tidal Control* was sitting lower in the water than it had been a moment ago, and its progress seemed to have stopped completely. Margo shrieked something from behind the wheel that Spencer couldn't hear, then abandoned steering altogether to run to the bow of the boat. She seemed to be yelling at them and at Ivan at the same time, but her threats were carried away by the wind and drowned out by the roaring of Bearhaven's speedboat's engine.

Margo's eyes landed on Spencer. The hair rose on his arms. He ducked, desperate to escape the nasty woman's hateful glare.

When Spencer lifted his head again, Evarita had finally put enough distance between the speedboat and the *Tidal Control* that Spencer couldn't make out Margo and Ivan's faces on their boat's deck anymore.

"*Now* we're losing them," Professor Weaver said as the speedboat crashed full speed across the water. "I thought they'd never go down!" the professor added.

"No kidding!" Evarita called back through the team's Ear-COMs. "Next time let's drill a bigger hole."

Drill a bigger hole?

"Wait a minute!" Spencer shouted. "What did you guys do to Margo and Ivan's boat?!"

"You didn't think we'd let you have all the fun, did you?" Evarita answered.

"If it came down to a chase—which it obviously did—we wanted to give ourselves as much of an advantage as possible," B.D. explained gruffly, as though squashing any ideas that they'd tampered with the *Tidal Control* just for the heck of it.

"Right, of course," Spencer answered, trying to sound businesslike. He couldn't help but smile. Sinking Margo and Ivan's boat was so cool. He cast a glance back in the *Tidal Control*'s direction and his smile faded. The boat was just a sinking shadow now, but Moon Farm loomed on the horizon, as threatening as ever. Spencer could still see the large illuminated silhouette of the painted bear on the stone wall surrounding the island. It looked like an enormous ghost. Spencer shuddered, remembering the words Pam had proclaimed loudly during his midnight assembly: "When we find Bearhaven, we'll be ready." He reached for his jade bear.

Bearhaven's team was going to escape tonight, that much was clear, but this battle wasn't over. Pam, Margo, Ivan, and their army of microchipped bears were coming for Bearhaven. Not today, and not on the *Tidal Control*, but they would finish this chase.

38

Spencer sat on the floor in the TUBE's wardrobe car as the train sped back toward Bearhaven. He was in the women's closet, his mission pack in his lap. The picture of himself with Mom and Dad in front of the Lab was on the floor in front of him. There wasn't a trace of the broken glass and frame he'd left behind after his confrontation with Yude on the way to Moon Farm. Spencer guessed Marguerite had removed it, leaving just the unframed picture behind.

Spencer was supposed to be getting himself cleaned up after the mission, but there was something he had to do first. In all the mayhem of their escape from Moon Farm, he hadn't had a single second to think back on seeing Uncle Mark in the tower. Now that Spencer was able to recall the moment he saw Uncle Mark, he realized there'd been clues his uncle had been at Moon Farm all along. First, there was the motorcycle, a perfect getaway vehicle parked in the very same parking lot Evarita had chosen for the ice cream truck. Then there was the silver dingy at the loading dock when Bearhaven's team arrived. Remembering the dingy made Spencer feel *way* better about the fact that it was only now occurring to him that he should have told Evarita to turn Bearhaven's boat around and return for Uncle Mark. The dingy would be all Uncle Mark needed to get back to shore. And lastly, the evidence that someone else had entered the illegal half of Moon Farm through the same skylight Spencer opened with a crowbar.

Spencer couldn't believe he hadn't put the pieces of the puzzle together sooner. But even if he'd figured out that Uncle Mark's solo mission had led him to Moon Farm, Spencer would never have predicted Uncle Mark would appear right when they needed him most.

There was no telling what would have happened to Spencer, Aldo, and Kate if the metal door of the shipping room had slammed shut, sealing them inside as the microchipped bear army approached. But how had Uncle Mark known they needed him? And where was Uncle Mark now?

What seemed like millions of questions started piling up in Spencer's mind.

He unzipped his mission pack and turned it over, dumping the contents onto the floor. He searched the pile of tools and emergency supplies for something unfamiliar. Whatever Uncle Mark had put in Spencer's mission pack was supposed to tell him everything he wanted to know.

Spencer pushed aside a Raymond's fuel bar and a roll of duct tape as he hunted for a notebook or a file. He moved a pair of scissors, a pair of gloves, and a small bundle of wires, but still couldn't find anything that looked out of place in the pile of mission materials. Then his eyes landed on a small red tin labeled "first aid kit." Spencer picked it up. He didn't remember seeing it before. He flipped open the top.

"Yes," he whispered to himself. An audio recorder was nestled inside. Spencer pulled it out, letting the empty tin fall into his lap. News about Mom and Dad was right here in his hands. Spencer didn't waste a single second. He pressed PLAY. Uncle Mark's voice filled the closet immediately.

"**Update**," Uncle Mark started. His voice was hushed. "**I located Pam's plane in Florida and followed it to Moon Farm. Margo, Ivan, Jane, and Shane were not on the plane. Dora was on the plane. Dora is kept with Pam at all times.**" There was a pause, then Uncle Mark spoke again. "**Update: Margo and Ivan have arrived at Moon Farm with Kate. They were sent to locate Bearhaven but could not. They brought Kate to Pam as consolation.**"

The audio recorder fell silent again. Spencer closed his eyes, waiting for more information. If Mom and Dad weren't on the plane with Pam, then where were they? As though answering Spencer's question, Uncle Mark's voice picked up again.

"**Update: Jane and Shane are not being held at Moon Farm. They are being held at Pam's personal headquarters. They are both being held there. Jane's cover was blown.**"

"No," Spencer whispered into the silence between Uncle Mark's updates. Now *both* of his parents were Pam's captives.

"**Update: Pam has left Moon Farm on a helicopter from the tower roof. He is going to his personal headquarters. I was not able to follow. He will be overseeing an assembly tonight by video.**" For a second, Spencer was angry. How could Uncle Mark let Pam get away? But then Uncle Mark spoke again.

"Update: I've located Pam's personal headquarters. Traced the origin of the video feed—what—" Suddenly, the audio recording picked up movement. Uncle Mark hadn't stopped taping, but it didn't sound as if he was paying attention to his update anymore. Spencer heard heavy footsteps. Uncle Mark was running. "Spencer!" he heard Uncle Mark call, but the voice was muffled. There was the sound of metal scraping against metal, then after a few more seconds, Uncle Mark's voice. "Hurry, Spence. You have to get out of here."

Spencer stopped the tape. His pulse was racing. Uncle Mark had been watching the midnight assembly and determining where the video feed was coming from when Pam's cameras turned on Spencer, Aldo, and Kate. He'd had to move so fast to help them he'd never stopped recording.

Spencer heard a bear enter the wardrobe car.

"Spencer?" It was B.D.

"I'm in here!" Spencer called. He set the tape recorder aside and scrambled to put the contents of his mission pack away. B.D. stepped into view in the closet's open doorway. The bear was much too large to enter with his whole body, but he moved his head inside, looking Spencer over.

"What's going on in here?" B.D. asked, inspecting the closet. When he turned his head, Spencer caught sight of the familiar furless patch at his jaw. Suddenly, Uncle Mark's words rushed into Spencer's head: *Dora was on the plane. Dora is kept with Pam at all times.*

Spencer gasped. It wasn't only his family who Uncle Mark had located. The jet-black bear with Pam during the midnight assembly was Dora, B.D.'s long-lost sister. Spencer had been so focused on news about Mom and Dad, Dora's name had barely registered.

"Well?" B.D. asked impatiently.

"B.D., there's something you have to hear." Spencer picked up the tape recorder. He rewound it all the way to the beginning, then held it between himself and B.D. and pressed PLAY.

"**Update.**" Uncle Mark's voice filled the closet once again. B.D.'s eyes flashed in surprise. He leaned in to hear Uncle Mark's report.

39

Spencer left B.D. in the wardrobe car and made his way to the medical car, trying to shake off his disappointment that Mom and Dad wouldn't be in Bearhaven when he got there. He knew it was good news that Uncle Mark had located Mom and Dad, but no matter how relieved Spencer was that Uncle Mark was getting closer to rescuing his parents, he also knew it would take yet another difficult mission to bring them home.

Spencer would be returning to Bearhaven without his family, and unless he repaired things with Kate, without a best friend, too. He opened the door to the medical car and stepped inside. The car was quiet.

"Hello, son," Professor Weaver said, startling Spencer. The bear was bent over a silver surgical table to one side of the car. A BEAR-COM and a variety of tools were scattered across the surface of the table.

"Hi." Spencer looked around the rest of the medical car. A curtain had been drawn across the car, closing off the back half. *Yude must be back there,* Spencer thought, hoping the drawn curtain wasn't a bad sign. In front of the curtain, on a bear-sized hospital bed, Kate was stretched out on her side, her back turned to Spencer. Marguerite and Evarita were with the cub. Marguerite sat back on her haunches, murmuring Ragayo as Evarita tended to Kate's ear.

"Will Kate be okay?" Spencer asked. Professor Weaver followed Spencer's gaze.

"I believe so. Her ear shouldn't need more than a few stitches."

Spencer shook his head, suddenly afraid that though Kate was safe, she'd never return to the playful, curious cub she used to be. "But will she be . . . *herself* again?"

"Yes, I think she will." Professor Weaver padded over to stand beside Spencer. "She's already on the mend, but it will take time."

"I'm so sorry," Spencer whispered, his voice wavering.

"It's all right, Spencer. I owe you an apology myself. We should have been more honest with you about the difficulty we were having in locating your parents. You deserve to know as much as anyone about their whereabouts." Professor Weaver paused. "Aldo reported that you saw your uncle at Moon Farm?"

Spencer nodded. "He gave me a tape with a bunch of information. B.D. has it now."

"Was there any news of your parents?"

"Pam is holding them—both Mom and Dad—at his private headquarters," Spencer said. "It's a different place than Moon Farm. Uncle Mark knows where it is."

"I see."

"Pam's really evil," Spencer blurted out. "He's after us, Professor Weaver. He's training a whole army of microchipped bears for when he finds Bearhaven, and they're getting close to finding it—it was Margo and Ivan who kidnapped Kate." Spencer pulled the jade bear out of his pocket. He rolled it over in his palm. "What if . . ." Spencer couldn't get the words out.

Professor Weaver understood anyway. "We're going to save your parents from Pam, Spencer." The bear's voice was determined. "We'll bring them home, son—"

"But *when*, Professor?" Spencer interrupted Professor Weaver. His frustration swelled. Evarita looked up from her work on Kate's ear. Spencer lowered his voice to a whisper. "I know Uncle Mark made progress, but there's still no way of knowing how long it will be before I see my family again."

Professor Weaver didn't answer right away. After what felt like an hour, the bear broke the silence. "You know, in Bearhaven, our definition of 'family' is entirely different than yours. Family is chosen and earned. Jane and Shane Plain may be *your* mother and father, but I think almost every bear in Bearhaven would say that they're their family, too. Spencer, almost every bear in Bearhaven would say that *you* are part of their family. You belong in Bearhaven just as much as any of us. We need you, Spencer. If we learned anything from this mission, it's that our work is only just beginning."

Spencer looked across the room at Kate. The cub lay perfectly still as Evarita bandaged her ear. Spencer remembered the day Kate taught him the Ragayo word *anbranda*. The bears used it for "friend," but Kate had explained it meant more than that. *Anbranda* meant "warrior for your family." If he and Kate hadn't been warriors for each other over the past few days, he didn't know *what* they were. And Spencer knew he'd do whatever he could to protect Kate and all the bears in Bearhaven from Pam.

Professor Weaver was right. These bears had become Spencer's family.

40

Spencer silent-walked through the passenger car. He didn't want to disturb B.D., who looked lost in thought as he stared out into the dark TUBE tunnel, or Aldo, who was fast asleep in one of the cocoon-like seats. Neither bear stirred when Spencer opened the door to the dining car and slipped through it.

Spencer chose a seat at the empty table. A moment later, the door opened. To Spencer's surprise, Kate padded in alone. The door closed behind her. The cub hesitated at the sight of Spencer. Her bandaged ear twitched. There was a BEAR-COM around her neck, but it wasn't hers. It wasn't pink and it didn't sparkle.

"Hi," Spencer said.

"Hi." Kate rose up onto her hind legs. She wobbled a little as she sniffed the air in front of her. "I thought I smelled—"

Just then, Marguerite pushed open the door and swept into the dining car. She set a tray piled high with salmon nuggets on the table in front of Spencer. "Salmon nuggets, anyone? I heard it was a certain cub's favorite dish."

Kate dropped to all fours and approached the table. Marguerite helped her into the seat across from Spencer. Once Kate was settled, Marguerite flashed all her teeth in a wide smile.

"Enjoy," she crooned, then she left the dining car.

The door closed behind Marguerite, leaving Spencer and Kate in silence. Spencer's stomach growled. The salmon nuggets smelled delicious.

Spencer cleared his throat. "I'm sorry," he said, his eyes locked on Kate.

Kate cocked her head to one side. She looked at Spencer.

"*Acha kunchaich,*" he said, careful to make the grunts and growls just as Yude had taught him, but he knew the Ragayo wasn't enough. He had to explain. "I never meant for anything bad to happen to you, Kate. I know you were protecting me when you jumped out of the woods, but I was trying to protect you, too. It was all just a big mistake and a bigger misunderstanding. I'm really, *really* sorry."

Kate dropped her head toward the table. She didn't look at Spencer for a moment. He wasn't sure if she was considering whether or not to accept his apology, or savoring the smell of the salmon nuggets.

Spencer's stomach growled. Kate's ears twitched at the sound. The cub lifted a claw to her BEAR-COM and switched it off.

"*Anbranda,*" she finally growled. She switched the translating device back on. "I forgive you, Spencer. You came to save me."

"*Anbranda,*" Spencer said back. He tried to keep his Ragayo from sounding like a cheer.

Kate speared a salmon nugget with her claw and brought it close to her face. She gave it a huge sniff. Spencer picked up a salmon nugget of his own. He smelled it just the way Kate had.

"Smells like home," he said, then popped it into his mouth whole.

Kate ate her salmon nugget in one bite. "Tastes like it, too." She reached for another nugget.

The door to the dining car swung open. A groggy-looking Aldo loped in, carrying a tray in his mouth. He set it down on the table by Spencer.

"I hope you aren't too full yet. I was told to deliver this to you," the bear said, taking a seat beside his sister.

"Peanut butter toast!" Spencer whooped. He dropped the salmon nugget in his hand and picked up a piece of his favorite food. He took a huge bite, savoring the sticky, delicious, crunchy peanut butter–covered toast.

Aldo speared Spencer's half-eaten salmon nugget and popped it into his own mouth.

Spencer put down his toast and picked up what he saw was placed on the tray beside the plate: his STORM training journal. "How did you—"

"I just delivered the tray, little man," Aldo cut in.

"I thought you'd like to have your journal back," Professor Weaver said, entering the car. He padded over to Kate and nuzzled her gently before taking a seat at the table. "After all, you'll need to continue your training once you get back to Bearhaven."

Spencer smiled, then filled his mouth with another big bite of peanut butter toast.

"How's Yude?" Aldo asked.

"He's going to be just fine," Professor Weaver answered. "He needs a great deal of stitches and a lot of rest. It will be some time before he's back to full strength, but Pinky will be able to give him all the care he needs. He will make a full recovery. Evarita and B.D. are with him now."

Spencer looked across the table at Kate. The cub's eyelids were drooping. She looked like she might fall asleep right there at the table. Aldo noticed, too. He gently headbutted his sister.

"Looks like we haven't gotten our Kate back just yet," he joked. "The cub I know would never fall asleep if there were salmon nuggets left to be eaten."

Kate gave a little shake of her fur. She reached for another salmon nugget sleepily.

"Hey, Kate," Spencer said. "Want me to show you how to use the seats in the passenger car? They have a special hood that you pull down and it turns into a bed. There's even a screen inside so you can play *Salmon King*!"

Kate nodded, her eyes wide. She glanced at the plate of salmon nuggets.

Professor Weaver chuckled. "I have a feeling your mother is going to feed you as many salmon nuggets as you want as soon as you get home, Kate. There's no need to polish off all of these." The professor stood up. He helped Kate down from her seat. "Why don't you take Spencer up on his offer to show you one of the TUBE's special seats?"

Spencer stood up and hurried around to lead the way into the passenger car. He could hear Kate, Aldo, and Professor Weaver padding along behind him.

Professor Weaver was definitely right. It may be a little while longer before Mom and Dad were free from Pam, but in the meantime, Bearhaven was exactly where Spencer belonged. He had family there. And with Pam, Margo, and the army of microchipped bears heading for Bearhaven, that family, his family, was going to need every single *anbranda* it had.

Property of SPENCER PLAIN

Class notes: Wilderness survival skills for bears

Teacher: Professor Spady

What to do if you see a human in the woods:

- The best way to deal with humans is to stay away! If you smell, hear, or see a human, leave the area as fast as possible!

- You may think the human has delicious food, like trash, birdseed, or pet food. But it's (NOT) worth the risk.

- Humans are unpredictable. Most humans will be just as scared as you are, but some humans are dangerous. It's hard to know which kind of human you are dealing with.

- If the human sees you, and doesn't leave immediately, show it that you want it to leave!

STEP 1: Swat the ground.

STEP 2: Make blowing and snorting noises.

STEP 3: Charge at the human, but don't get too close. You may be able to scare it away by pretending you're going to attack.

STEP 4: If the human runs away, don't chase it. Even if you're curious about the human,
do not get closer.

STEP 5: If the human gets closer to you, you may be dealing with an aggressive or unintelligent human. Leave the area quickly—run!

Ragayo Words:

Abragan = for the bears

Acha kunchaich = I'm sorry / I didn't know my own strength

Anbranda = friend / warrior for your family

Shala = safe

Val = home

Learn more about the bears of Bearhaven, and continue the adventure with Spencer and Kate at www.secretsofbearhaven.com.

EGG IN THE HOLE PRODUCTIONS THANKS:

Erin Black for her valuable editorial guidance, and Nancy Mercado, David Levithan, and Ellie Berger for their support.

Ross Dearsley for his gorgeous illustrations, Nina Goffi for her talented book design, and Rebekah Wallin for creating books from manuscripts.

For applying their creative marketing talent to Bearhaven: Bess Braswell, Jazan Higgins, Lori Benton, Saraceia Fennell, Antonio Gonzalez, and Michelle Campbell.

For their enthusiastic and ongoing expert advice and contributions to the world of Bearhaven: Dr. Thomas Spady, Bear Biologist, California State University San Marcos; and Dr. Sherri Wells-Jensen, Linguist, Bowling Green State University.

Louisa Gummer, for bringing the voice of Bearhaven to life.

Emma D. Dryden and Elizabeth Grojean, for ongoing editorial and managerial creativity, support, and enthusiasm.

EGG IN THE HOLE
PRODUCTIONS

Egg in the Hole Productions creates rich worlds and memorable characters that draw kids back again and again into series they love.

www.egginthehole.com

ABOUT THE AUTHOR

K. E. Rocha is the author of *Secrets of Bearhaven*, developed in collaboration with Egg in the Hole Productions. She received a BA in English from Trinity College and an MFA from New York University. She has never visited with talking bears, although she often talks to her goofy little hound dog, Reggie, while writing in her studio in Queens, New York.